IF NOT
FOR YOU

IF NOT FOR YOU

•

JOYE AMES

AVALON BOOKS
THOMAS BOUREGY AND COMPANY, INC.
401 LAFAYETTE STREET
NEW YORK, NEW YORK 10003

PRINTED IN THE UNITED STATES OF AMERICA
ON ACID-FREE PAPER
BY HADDON CRAFTSMEN, BLOOMSBURG, PENNSYLVANIA

For Joan and Tere'—we will always love you

Chapter One

Somewhere in the skies between Pittsburgh and the North Carolina coast, Dana convinced herself that she was having a case of nervous anxiety brought on by thinking about Jeff Satterfield and *Blockade Runner* Cruises.

Once she finished with that problem, everything else would fall into place. Once she got that irascible man out of her mind, her life would go back to being the placid sea it had always been until the moment she met him.

Had it only been a year since she'd faced "that man" and weathered those icy gray eyes and that bone-chilling blast of anger?

How many times during that year had she called him and been told that he was out? He never returned her calls. When he had applied for another loan to do repairs on his schooner, a red flag had popped out on the computer.

Since *Blockade Runner* was one of her loan decisions for the bank, it was up to Dana to make sure the bank didn't lose out on their investment.

She could recall reading through the well-written proposal for the cruise that would take happy tourists through the waters Blackbeard the pirate had once frequented off the coast of North Carolina. The money was right. The plan was well thought out. The man was an experienced ship's captain with references from one of the world's biggest luxury cruise lines.

When she'd visited the operation a month after the loan approval, the *Blockade Runner*'s owner had been rude, arrogant, and impossible to handle.

He was of the opinion that since the bank had loaned him the money to start his cruise business, they should back off and let him run it. Dana had done her best to explain that she wanted to help him. Jeff Satterfield had intimated that she shouldn't let the door hit her on the way out.

The result was a stalemate. Satterfield had stalked away to his boat. Dana had waited in vain for him to return, finally flying back to Pittsburgh.

Her report was written very differently. She didn't know how to admit that she had let the man beat her because she couldn't stand to see those swaying masts or that moving water.

The Ellers were originally a sailing family that had settled down and founded a bank to help other sailing families make a living from their trade. The elder members of her family were all born with seawater in their veins. The family tradition had bypassed Dana.

Then there was that other thing.

It was something she'd tried not to think about but it still lurked in the back of her mind.

Jeff Satterfield had kissed her.

Oh, it had been a mistake. Both of them had acknowledged that fact. He had apologized politely and she had assured him that it was nothing.

It had all happened innocently enough. She had arrived at the start of his birthday party. He had mistaken her for someone else. Who, she was never quite clear about afterwards.

But when he had walked into the office and seen her waiting, he'd slid his hands over her eyes from behind and told her to guess who.

"I'm waiting for Jeff—"

"Lucky guy," he murmured near her ear.

He'd turned her to face him and before she could speak, he'd laid his mouth on hers.

When she thought back on that moment, she knew it shouldn't have been something that stayed with her for the year. She should have simply put it out of her mind.

She wasn't unattractive, she considered logically. Men had made passes at her before.

Still, it wasn't the fact that he'd kissed her that bothered her. It was her response.

At first, she'd been too stunned to protest. Every thought flew out of her head and her brain shut down at their retreat.

By the time she'd registered what was happening, she'd found herself standing on tiptoe and her arms had been wrapped around his neck. She'd dropped her briefcase without realizing it.

Another man had interrupted them before a troop of well-wishers had stormed in for his birthday party. Then he had introduced them.

Dana had been intensely embarrassed. The crowd had separated them but not before she saw the look of shock and amazement that had passed Jeff's rugged features.

Jeff had looked at her with those stormy eyes from across the room. The intensity of his gaze had scalded her. Even while his friends were congratulating him and making jokes about his age, he had been looking at her.

The scent of his aftershave had been on her hands and the fresh air and salty tang of the sea had lingered in her senses. It had all happened so quickly. She hadn't had time to think. But she was honest enough to concede that she had been embarrassed . . . and very intrigued.

She hadn't told Branden about the kiss. It had seemed childish. What would she have said? A man I've never met kissed me and made me forget everything for a moment?

She and Branden had a good relationship. She trusted him. He trusted her. They were right for each other. Their careers were headed in the same direction.

But she hadn't felt right since she'd realized that she was going to have to fly down to the coast and deal with that man again. It might have been a year since she'd seen him last but his face was as vivid to her as if she'd been there yesterday. That scent of his aftershave still clung to her and his kiss still haunted her.

The whole thing was ridiculous! She sounded like she was infatuated with the man. In reality, he'd made her look like a fool. She dreaded the confrontation she knew was waiting for her. It had taken her weeks to get over her last encounter with Jeff Satterfield.

It was the thought of failure, she told herself. It wasn't that stupid kiss. She was too mature, too professional to let something like that bother her.

True, it had bothered her for a short time. It had embarrassed her that she had kissed a stranger so . . .

passionately. Even thinking about her response made her uncomfortable.

But it wasn't the kiss!

She was a good judge of character. She had never had to withdraw her recommendation for a loan. She was proud of that fact. Marine Bank of Pittsburgh had never lost money on any of her accounts.

For the first time, she had cause to doubt that rock-steady composure and level-headed sense of judgment. It was only natural that her hands were a little shaky and her stomach felt uncomfortably tight at the thought of letting everyone down.

Solving the problem, at least in the confines of her own mind, Dana pushed the image of ''that man'' from her thoughts.

She thought about Branden and decided that they should set a date for their marriage. After a three-year engagement, it was time to make it permanent. The timing would never be better.

She yawned and closed her eyes, picturing everything in her mind. They would have a lovely wedding, possibly the following year. In the spring. They would have at least two smiling children who were well mannered and intelligent. A boy and a girl. They would have a beautiful house and a successful life. And they would be enormously happy together.

But in her dreams, as she slept restlessly on the short flight, they were married on the slippery deck of a high-masted schooner. Her nemesis was performing the ceremony.

"Hold on," Jeff Satterfield told her. "It's going to be a rough ride!"

Dana reached for Branden's hand, but a wave had washed him overboard. Her beautiful white wedding dress was soaking wet. She looked down at the frothy sea for some sign of her fiancé, but the tide had taken him.

He was gone. The gray sea was empty. When she looked back at Jeff Satterfield, his eyes were the same color as the water. He held out his hand to her and she shook her head, jumping over the rail herself before he could reach her.

The cold, rolling water was coming up in her face and she was starting to gasp for air, when the pilot announced that they had touched ground in Wilmington, North Carolina.

"Rough ride?" the woman beside her asked as the plane taxied in for a landing. Her child was still asleep on her lap.

Dana shuddered and nodded her head.

Half an hour later, she walked through the airport, past the luggage carousel. She carried her only bag.

She didn't need more than that to do her job. The sooner she reached the *Blockade Runner*'s office and faced Jeff Satterfield, the sooner she could be on a plane bound for home.

Back in time for dinner with Branden and making

plans for the rest of their lives together. The perfect ones. Not the ones that involved schooners and jumping into the water.

It was after noon when she walked out into the warm coastal sunshine. The difference in climates was immediate. In Pittsburgh, it was coming to the end of the long winter, but it was still cold. Her heavy coat was suffocating her as she left the plane in Wilmington.

On the milder coast of North Carolina, spring was already in full bloom. The warm ocean breezes drifted across the new green leaves. Red tulips, her mother's favorite, danced gaily in the wind outside the airport. Bright yellow daffodils held their heads proudly.

Dana dropped her briefcase on the sidewalk outside the main terminal building and took off her coat. Her gray suit had made the trip without a wrinkle. Careful shopping, her mother had always told her. That was her travel secret. She touched a hand to her hair, but the well-cut style was in place, despite the wind that whipped around the building.

Taking a deep breath, Dana was prepared to meet the enemy.

A few feet away, a yellow taxi swerved close to the sidewalk and a tall, unnaturally thin man eased himself out of the cab. "Need a ride, ma'am?"

Dana looked at the cab. It had definitely seen better days.

The man lit a cigarette, coughed a little, then smiled down at her.

"I need to get out to the docks, but I'll need a ride back later," she told him, making up her mind. "How much?"

He looked her over quickly, as though assessing how much she could afford to pay. The smoke from his cigarette blew across the space between them, drifting in the breeze.

"Thirty dollars. But you buy dinner if we stay past four."

It was high and she knew it. The man was dressed like a scarecrow and driving a car that seemed destined to fall apart. And he was taking advantage of her. But there was no sign of another cab being offered and taking a cab would be faster than renting a car.

"Great." She nodded, tossing her coat in the car as he opened the door. He put her case in beside her and climbed behind the wheel, obviously not at home with wearing a seat belt.

"Where to?" he asked, looking at her in the rearview mirror. His head grazed the ceiling.

"Front Street," she answered dourly, fastening her own seat belt. "Jeff Satterfield's place. *Blockade Runner* Cruises. Do you know it?"

"Sure." He shrugged. "He's got a nice little operation out there."

With an effort, Dana kept herself from nervously

fingering the patch behind her ear. Just the mention of the sea was almost enough to make her turn green. It was too late to turn back.

"Goin' out with him?" he asked. "Chartered?"

"No." Dana shook her head vehemently, swinging her neat auburn cap of hair. "No. Just business."

"Used to go shrimpin' with his father," the driver told her, using one lean hand to guide the steering wheel, almost lying back in his seat. "Jeff's a good boy."

A good boy? Dana turned her head to look out the window, watching the long stretches of marshland pass on the nearly deserted road. Thinking of Jeff Satterfield as a boy was too much a stretch for her imagination. A demon. A madman. Maybe a rudely independent fool. Surely that face had never been young and innocent!

There was a frightening intensity to the long reaches of lowland and the level, boundless sweep of water. It was as though it would be all too easy to be dragged away. Nothing seemed to end and yet everything could be swallowed up and gone forever.

"Is it much farther?" she asked, just to say something, anything.

"Not too much," came the nondescript reply.

"Are you driving the speed limit?" she wondered aloud. The car appeared to be barely moving along the road.

"Been drivin' this road near forty years. I'll get you there."

Great, she thought, but didn't reply out loud. *But will it be sometime today?*

She recalled the *Blockade Runner*'s offices being in the historic district along the river. It was a picturesque area with cobblestone streets and antique wooden structures. Roughly hewn by sea breezes, the shops and offices faced the waterway, creating an elegant atmosphere.

When the driver had circled the block twice without any luck finding a parking place, Dana asked him to stop and let her out.

"If you could come back in an hour," she suggested hopefully.

"Sure thing." He nodded and winked. "Think that'll be enough time?"

"More than enough." She hauled her briefcase out of the car with an impatient hand. She was at a loss about her heavy coat, however, hating to drag it with her.

"I'll just bring it back when I come," he suggested.

"Won't you be picking up another fare?" she wondered.

"Nah." He laughed. "I'm retired. I try to limit myself to one a day. You're it."

"Okay." She smiled a little at his words. It wasn't just the view that was blurred around the edges in that place, she thought. The people were a little hard to define as well.

Dana thanked him, made sure he was wearing a watch, and started up the walk that ran along the Cape Fear River.

Fishing boats vied with launches that offered to take passengers across the river. A sign, marked down from six dollars to four dollars, offered shore-line sight-seeing cruises on a small boat that was painted bright red and black.

Dana reached the *Blockade Runner*'s offices, clutched her case a little tighter, then pushed open the door and walked inside.

It was a working office, a little chipped at the edges, a little worn and dirty. The money lay in the cruises leaving the deep harbor of Wilmington, however, not in the decor of the office few travelers would ever see as part of their journey.

"Excuse me." A man walked past her carrying a box filled haphazardly with papers.

"I'm looking for Jeff Satterfield," Dana said as he passed her, recognizing him from a year before.

"Not here," the man, dark-haired, his face a mass of tanned wrinkles, told her bluntly.

Dana fumed. If they thought they could put her off again, they were going to be disappointed.

A young girl was talking on an old black tele-phone. Her long hair was dark brown and slightly curly and her eyes, when she looked up at Dana, were sky blue.

"Can I help you?" she asked, pausing on the phone and in the middle of her *Seventeen* magazine.

"I'm Dana Eller. I'm looking for—"

"Jeff." The girl flashed her a quick smile.

"Yes." Dana smiled. "I don't think we met last year."

"Probably not. I'm Penny Satterfield."

"Satterfield?" Dana was visibly surprised.

"His sister. He's not here."

Dana counted to ten. "Where is he?"

"Down at the *Runner*," she replied evenly.

"How do I get there from here?" Dana asked persistently.

"Oh. Well . . ."

"Look, Penny," Dana began, ready to do battle.

"Somethin' wrong?" the man she'd passed coming into the office stopped and asked.

"I need to talk with Jeff Satterfield." She attempted to keep her tone as neutral as possible. "I've just flown down from Pittsburgh and I'm not going to go away without seeing him! He can't continue to hide from the bank if he wants to keep going as a customer. Surely he can see that?"

"Sure." He shrugged, grabbing another box. "I can take you down there."

"What?" Dana demanded on a weak note, some of the wind spiked from her sails.

He started toward the door, a box on his hefty shoulder. "You can ride down with me." He walked across the street to where an old pickup truck was parked. After depositing the box he'd carried from the office into the back, he held out a dirty hand to her.

"Mattie Ames." He smiled. "Jeff's assistant."

Dana felt her face heat up as she remembered the man breaking up their embrace. She had only seen him briefly after that desperate moment, not really enough time for an introduction. She put her hand in his.

"Dana Eller, Marine Bank of Pittsburgh. I remember you. Can't we wait here for Mr. Satterfield?"

"He won't be coming back to the office for a few days," Mattie told her calmly, his face as unruffled as a windless sea.

Dana was prepared for that treatment. "His loan will be recalled if he doesn't talk to me. He won't get the money to fix his boat."

Mattie shrugged. "That's part of the problem. Jeff's had to give up this office as of today. We're just cleaning everything out."

Dana bit her lip, her stomach tensing. "So, he's—"

"—moved his office to the *Runner*." Mattie nodded as though it was the most natural thing in the world. "I'm taking this stuff down there right now."

"Maybe we could meet somewhere?" she suggested hopefully.

Mattie shook his head. "He can't leave the *Runner* right now. Between moving everything and working on those engine repairs . . ."

"All right." She swallowed hard. "All right. I'll ride down there with you."

"Okay. If you're ready . . . ?"

"I'm ready," she determined, hoping her anger and her seasickness patch could sustain her. "Let's go."

The old red pickup truck went no faster than the taxi she'd taken from the airport. They crawled down the streets, turning along side streets when Mattie had the urge. He was a determined and well-informed tour guide, pointing out the old governor's house, telling her the ghost stories associated with the naval war memorial.

"Wilmington was just about the only Confederate port to stay open during the War Between the States, you know," he said, one arm crooked out the window, smiling at her.

"I didn't realize," she returned politely.

"Yeah, the Yankees couldn't ever shut her down. That's where the blockade runners came in. They brought in food and contraband that couldn't come in any other way. Fastest ships in the world."

"That's why you chose the name for your company?" she encouraged, glad at least to have someone talking to her. The last time, they had acted as though she had the plague.

"Jeff was always fascinated with them," he explained. "His family goes back that far here, and on the barrier islands. Have you been out there yet?"

"No," she admitted quietly. "Water . . ."

"Yeah," he recalled, "you and water don't mix so well."

The sun glinted off of the river, turning the horizon to gold. There was heavy water traffic. Tall sailing ships maneuvered around freighters and ferries, smaller passenger boats carefully making way for the larger vehicles.

Dana cleared her throat and looked away from the hypnotic sight of the water to her companion's face. "Is Mr. Satterfield taking out a cruise tonight?"

"Nope." Mattie turned right and proceeded down the tiny side street. "Until we have that engine up to the mark, the best we can manage is around the harbor."

"So you've had a serious loss of income?" she asked, trying to keep her mind occupied with those things she could understand.

Mattie shrugged and laughed easily. "I don't keep up with that stuff, Miss Eller. Jeff and I went fishin' one day. He says to me, 'Mattie, want to start a cruise business?' and I said, 'Sure.' "

Dana laughed. "That simple?"

"That simple," he confirmed.

"Have you known each other a long time?" she

questioned, watching the white gulls spin around a tall church spire.

"All our lives," he answered, bringing the truck to an unexpected stop. "Here we are."

Dana looked out of her window, and there was the *Blockade Runner*. It was nudging the side of a wide dock, the letters freshly painted in black on her shining white hull. Even though she'd read the specifications on the craft, it was much bigger there in the dark water than she'd anticipated. It was like a small floating house. The big sails were lashed at the masts; the brass fittings shone in the afternoon sun.

It was a beautiful piece of craftsmanship. The lines were as smooth and flowing as the water that would carry it. It was an observation that Dana suddenly realized she could never have made before that day.

She felt her stomach tense as she watched the craft bob up and down in the water. She stepped out of the truck fearfully, putting her feet down carefully on the wooden dock. The wood was washed gray with sun and water, wet from a small, late-morning thunderstorm.

She stood, not moving, watching the river and the boat beside her, feeling the movement of the dock. The wind blew through her hair, feathering it lightly against her neck. From overhead, a few gulls played, calling into the wind.

"You okay?" Mattie asked as he walked past her to the back of the truck and picked up a box of files.

The movement broke the strange spell that had engulfed Dana. She shook her head. Everything was fine. It took that long for her to grasp the importance of what she was, or rather wasn't, experiencing.

She wasn't sick. She clutched her case to her side, tightened her grip on reality, and slammed the truck door shut.

"I'm fine," she assured Mattie with a bright smile.

While she could feel that rolling sensation in the pit of her stomach, she wasn't actually getting sick. Without the seasickness patch, she knew she would be running for the tree line at the end of the dock.

Mattie wavered uncertainly. "Uh, that's great. Jeff should be around here somewhere."

"Let me help you," Dana offered, grabbing a smaller box from the back of the pickup and following him to the boarding plank.

There was a bad moment as she was crossing the less-than-reassuring plank that connected the boat to the dock. She looked down into the water swirling between the dock and the boat and was uncertain. But she put one foot in front of the other. Her grasp was white-knuckled on the box of paper, her brief-case firmly on the top.

"Jeff!" Mattie called as he hit the deck an instant before her.

There was no reply. Mattie ducked his head down to pass under the doorway that led into the cabin area of the boat.

Dana followed him, looking around herself at the tidy berths through the other open doors. The furniture was simple, but adequate. The whole place smelled of salt air and lemon polish.

"Jeff?" Mattie called out again.

Dana felt her temper beginning to rise. If this was some game they were playing . . .

"Down here!" She finally heard an unmistakable voice. Jeff Satterfield.

"What's goin' on?" Mattie asked ahead of her.

"I think I might have found the problem," Jeff answered with a laugh. "Where's Ms. Eller? Did she make it down to the dock or did you have to leave her on the hill?"

"Jeff . . ." Mattie tried to warn, putting down his box.

"I've seen a lot of people get seasick in my time, Mattie," Jeff continued, "but that woman turned three shades of green just looking at the water! I don't think she can chase me down here!"

Dana slammed down the box she held, shaking the small desk she abused.

"Jeff." Mattie sighed.

Jeff stopped on the stairs coming up from the engine room. He wiped the grease from his hands and looked up. He met Dana's angry eyes with laughter that died quickly from his face.

"It looks as though everything's here," Dana said, glancing over the computer and boxes of files in the office. "Suppose we get started?"

Chapter Two

""Ms. Eller," Jeff Satterfield acknowledged her presence. He darted a quick look at Mattie, who shrugged and sauntered out of the cabin, leaving them alone.

"Mr. Satterfield," Dana responded calmly.

"How was your flight?" he wondered, tossing the rag he'd held into a nearby bucket.

"Unnecessary," she answered, letting a little of the anger she couldn't quite swallow come to the surface. "Why haven't you returned my calls?"

"I've been working long hours," he explained, running his hand through his hair. "I can't always be there waiting for you to call."

"Then what about replying to my letters?" she

demanded. "If you didn't have the time, surely your secretary could have answered?"

"Now, just a minute." Jeff stood a head above her, a line of black grease across his tanned cheek. "There's no reason for you to take it out on Penny."

"There's no reason to take it out on anyone," Dana shot back at him, a faint flush stealing across her face.

He was taller than she'd remembered. Strange. She thought she had stored away every detail about him. Those cold gray eyes staring down at her, trying to bore holes in her brain. Those she had recalled quite accurately.

She realized that she was losing control of the situation and took a deep breath, looking away from him. There had to be some way to make him realize that she was on his side. She had as much to lose as he did in his business.

"Look." She tried another tack. "I want to help you. I don't want you to lose your schooner."

"You've got a funny way of showing it," he told her flatly.

"I went to bat for you last year," she reminded him. "My reputation is on the line here with you every day. If you fail, it means I didn't do my job right."

Dana considered, as she looked at him, that his eyes were the color of an angry sea. He was a little dirty. His dark brown hair stood on end from running impatient fingers through it. The high cheekbones and wide, mobile mouth were the same. He was as she had remembered him, devastatingly angry.

"I tried to tell you last year, Jeff, but you wouldn't listen," she explained patiently. "You own your own business, but the bank expects to help you keep up with it. When you have a problem, we have a problem. We want you to do well with your cruises."

Jeff stared down at her, hostility making his back stiff. Something about this woman made his teeth hurt. He just plain wanted to pick her up and throw her overboard. That nice neat fringe of red hair and those wide green eyes. Those soft, pink lips . . .

"I tried to tell you last year, *Dana*." He expressed his anger in her name. "I don't want your help. I can handle the *Runner* and everything at this end."

"And we're supposed to be waiting at your beck and call, asking how much do you need, sir?" she finished recklessly.

"You're supposed to give me enough room to breathe," he protested. "I'm doing the best I can trying to make it all work out."

"I don't want to be here any more than you want me to be," she threw back at him. "If you would have answered one phone call or sent me one short note, explaining why you never make your payments on time, I would be at home right now."

They stood together in the close confines of the stateroom, their anger electrifying the moist air that floated in from the deck. The blare of a deep horn from some passing vessel filled the silence between them.

"You want to know why my payments are late? You want to sort through the whole mess yourself?" he questioned, his eyes darting over her softly curved face.

"Yes!"

"Well then, I think you should do that," he told her roughly. "You want to help? Then sit down right here and you tell me why there isn't enough money. I have to get the *Runner* out there or there won't be *any* money."

Dana shook her head. "I'm not here as your accountant—"

"My accountant?" He laughed. "I had to fire him six months ago after I caught him helping himself to the profits."

"Then surely—"

"What?" he asked. "You said it mattered to you. Well, here's your chance to prove it."

She looked at the boxes of mangled papers.

"Ignore the stuff in the boxes," he said, impatient with himself that he felt a little guilty bringing her down there, hoping she'd get sick. "Everything's in the computer."

Dana knew from the look on his face that he thought she would turn him down. It wasn't her job.

But she was there to convince him that they were a partnership.

"All right," she replied, stubbornly unwilling for him to see her back down. "I'll do what I can."

"Wonderful!" He smiled unpleasantly. "I'll do what *I* can."

He started to walk away while Dana cleared the box and a pair of dirty socks from the chair in front of the computer. The room was a mess, probably made more so by the lack of organized space.

It was obviously his private quarters, since it lacked all of the tidy reassurance of the rest of the boat. Engine parts warred with plastic cases and large pieces of canvas.

She took off her gray suit jacket and hung it on the back of the chair, glancing at her watch. The last plane out was at 6:00 P.M. She would have to do what she could before then.

Jeff paused halfway down the ladder to the engine area, about to speak again, when she began to take off her jacket. He watched in fascination, his eyes appreciating the soft sophistication and slender figure of the woman in the cool white silk blouse and gray skirt.

There was no mistaking the nice-sized diamond on the finger of her left hand, either. Somewhere back in Pittsburgh, there was a man who was waiting for her.

There was a woman beneath that gray wool armor,

he mused, watching her take her seat at the computer. The light from the porthole caught at the fiery highlights in her hair.

Not for the first time in that long year since he'd met her, he recalled their first meeting. The moment when their lips had met and there had been a spark of fire between them.

It had surprised him. Especially once he'd realized who she was and why she was there. Yet even while they had warred, that kiss had burned in his memory.

Dana realized that she had not asked him how to log on to his system.

"Jeff," she called, turning to find him at floor level, his eyes casually appraising her.

"Yes, Dana?" he queried innocently.

"Your password?" She frowned, feeling self-conscious.

"Just press F2 and enter HITNRUN under *Blockade Runner*," he advised. "That'll get you in."

"Thank you." She turned her back to him pointedly. "I think I can handle it from here."

"I'm sure you can," he muttered, grunting as he bumped his head on the top of the ladder.

Dana smiled, then concentrated fiercely on the computer monitor, ignoring his quick oath as he disappeared below.

"So?" Mattie asked, crouching down low in the engine room. He glanced significantly at the ceiling. "What gives?"

"Who knows?" Jeff responded, picking up a wrench where he'd left it. "Let's crank this over, Mattie."

"Sure," Mattie answered, going topside and passing Dana, who pored over the figures on the computer screen. Whatever was going on, they didn't intend to share it with him.

The afternoon passed quickly. Dana stayed on the computer. Mattie alternated between the engine room and the upper deck, running when Jeff yelled to start or stop the engine.

About 4:00 P.M, there were footsteps on the boarding plank, followed by a whiff of vanilla.

"Jeff," Penny called, descending lightly to the deck. "Mattie? Is the wicked witch gone— Oh, sorry!"

Dana blinked her eyes behind her plain-rimmed glasses. She smiled as bright red suffused the girl's thin face.

"No," she told her. "She's still here."

"I'm sorry, Ms. Eller." Penny tried to find the words but there were none that could fit the occasion. "Is Jeff—?" She glanced at the hole in the floor.

"I think so," Dana answered, carefully moving her stiff neck. She looked at her watch, stunned by the time that had passed. She had managed to do a great deal in the time, but there was so much more to do.

"Jeff?" Penny lowered herself carefully through the hatch.

"Penny?" Jeff glanced up at her from his vantage point under the engine. "Is it that late already?"

"I just came by to see about supper."

"Great," he replied without looking up. "Go and get something to eat. A couple of pizzas or something. You know where the petty cash is."

"Make it anchovy," Mattie yelled out from an unseen depth.

"Get something else, too, Penny—extra cheese, or mushroom," Jeff countermanded. "She's only twelve, Mattie. She doesn't have your cast-iron stomach."

"What about her?" Penny whispered, rolling her eyes toward the ceiling.

"Her?" Jeff asked, then recalled his uninvited guest. "Is she still here?"

She nodded silently.

"Yeah, get something for her, too."

"No." Penny made a face. "What's she doing?"

"Just get something to eat, honey," Jeff finished wearily. "And don't worry about it."

Penny climbed back out, watching briefly as Dana took apart a file on the computer with a low growl coming from the back of her throat.

"Uh, Jeff said to get something to eat. Do you want something?"

"I think little children are hard to get this time of year," Dana answered without looking up at the girl.

Penny thought about it. There was no immediate reply.

Dana smiled. "Never mind. Whatever's fine, thanks."

Mattie ran through the room and up the stairs just after the girl left.

The engine turned over, starting briefly, then switched off with a low rumble. Jeff roared from under the floor at her feet. Dana shook her head and went into another file.

Penny returned promptly with several pizzas and a case of canned sodas. She called down into the engine room for Jeff and Mattie, then went on deck without saying a word to Dana.

Dana rubbed her tired eyes under her glasses. She stretched her back and shoulders as she stood up. It was nearly 5:00 P.M.

She decided to have a slice of pizza and something to drink, then a brief consultation with Jeff Satterfield before she tried to find a ride to the airport.

It was then that she remembered the man in the cab who still had her coat. Obviously, it was going to cost her for dinner.

She logged off the computer and went on deck, finding a seat near the rail with a can of soda and a piece of cheese pizza. It was good to be out in the fresh air after being cramped in the cabin for so long.

The harbor was busy around them. A cruise ship from Brazil was leaving a wide wake as it trailed the setting sun, while several smaller vessels followed down the wide river way.

"I told Earl that you'd be down here," Penny said in a quiet voice. She was embarrassed and uncomfortable in Dana's company.

"Earl?" Dana asked, swallowing a bite of pizza.

"The cab driver who brought you down to the office. He said you owed him dinner."

"Thanks," Dana answered. "Do you know his number? I can call him . . ."

"Are you leaving?" Penny's attitude picked up at once.

Dana nodded, hearing the change in her voice. "The last plane out is six P.M."

"It's Earl's Cab in the yellow pages." Penny brushed pizza from her hands in a satisfied manner. "I'm not sure about the number."

Mattie and Jeff joined them on the deck. Grease-smeared faces and clothes aside, they dug into the pizza.

Dana watched Jeff take a bite of his pizza, drink a little soda, then wipe the dirt from his face with an old rag. His thoughts were still in the boat's hull with the engine that didn't want to run.

She reluctantly admitted a certain fascination with the man's active features. He had the most expressive face. His eyes spoke volumes of anger and frustration. Not handsome in a classical sense, there was something very appealing about him in a rugged, individual manner.

Dana looked away when he looked up, but not fast enough. He'd felt her eyes on him.

"I can't believe you're still here," he confessed promptly. "Are you ready to report me to the IRS now?"

Dana finished her can of soda and took off her glasses. "It's a wonder to me they haven't already picked you up," she answered seriously. "Your books are a mess."

Mattie snickered, tossing Jeff another piece of pizza. "He never was much good at math."

"You need a good accountant," Dana continued. "Someone to keep your records in order for you."

"Can't the bank do that?" Jeff wondered sarcastically.

"I can see that you need help." Dana ignored the jibe. "But your receipts are good. Up and running, you'll be fine."

"Up and running," Jeff replied darkly.

Dana stood up, putting her empty can into a trash container attached to the deck. "I'm going to recommend that we loan you what you've asked, plus enough for a good accountant for a year. And enough to keep you on your feet. You need your office back again."

Mattie crushed his aluminum can and tossed it into the trash, sharing a black look with Jeff and Penny.

"I have to get going," Penny lied. "I have to go to the library."

"Okay, honey." Jeff hugged her despite her squeals of protest. "Thanks for your help."

"You're welcome," she retorted, trying to make sure none of the grease had come off on her. "Do you want me to send Earl for you, Ms. Eller?"

"That would be great." Dana nodded. "Let me get my things."

"Are you going?" Jeff stood up, thinking how much his companions had begun to look like rats deserting a sinking ship. And how much he felt like he deserved it. The woman was going to come through for him. Again.

"My plane leaves at six." Dana looked at her watch, seeing that she had barely enough time to catch it.

"Earl's waiting for her," Penny put in quickly.

"I'll take you out there," Jeff offered.

"You need to stay and work on your boat," Dana protested.

Mattie shook his head. "Earl will never get you there in time." They all agreed.

"But he has my coat," Dana began, wondering what had prompted the sudden offer and the lessening of that thundercloud that she'd come to know as Jeff's face.

"We'll just get it from him and go on from there," he promised. "Give me a minute."

Penny left, wishing Dana a good flight after Jeff disappeared below. Mattie went down to tinker with the engine a little more before he left for the night.

Dana stood at the rail, looking out at the wide expanse of the harbor, trying to follow the river to the point where it would meet the sea.

It had been quite an experience. Sitting on a boat all day, eating pizza in the open air with the gulls flying above her head.

Maybe it was a fluke, but it was as though finding herself suddenly able to enjoy the water, she longed to head out of that harbor. She watched the Brazilian ship disappearing, knowing it would reach the open waters quickly.

"Here's your jacket."

Dana wondered where that bit of yearning had been hiding in her head. She blinked her eyes and looked at Jeff.

He had changed clothes and looked almost presentable, she thought, appreciating the clean if slightly tattered blue jeans. His white shirt was open at his brown throat and she watched the pulse beat there in a steady rhythm.

"Thanks," she answered, looking away from the spot and turning her back on the inviting water.

"Look," he began as they walked across the plank

to the dock. "I'm not really good at apologizing, but . . ."

"That's all right." She smiled slightly, not looking down at the water. "Neither am I."

"Great." He grinned. "Maybe we can go from here?"

He offered her his hand and she put hers into it, giving it a firm shake as her grandfather had always taught her.

His hand was roughly callused, but had a warm strength that she found herself reluctant to release. She looked down at it, wondering how he had been able to clean up so quickly.

"I know it was pretty messy back there." He saw her glance and self-consciously moved his hand. "I clean up pretty well though."

"Very well," she agreed as he held up his hands for her inspection.

The old truck started easily, making much better time away from the docks than Mattie had made coming down the hill.

They found Earl sleeping in his cab at the corner, and Jeff tucked thirty dollars into his pocket. He took her coat out of the backseat without waking the man.

"That was pretty generous," he told Dana when he handed her the heavy coat. "Old Earl will raise his rates on us now."

"He said I owed him supper."

"That meant a burger down at Lacey's for a dollar

and a cup of coffee.'' Jeff laughed, starting the truck back in motion. ''I think he can afford that on what you paid him.''

The drive through town was mostly silent, the sun already starting to drift low in the horizon. Church steeples rose up from the city, piercing the fading sky.

''A week or so and you would have seen the azaleas,'' Jeff told her as they passed the bushes sporting thousands of tight red buds. They were laid out in a centerpiece that surrounded the sign that read *Welcome to Wilmington, North Carolina.*

''Maybe I'll come back for a cruise someday,'' she replied in an unconsciously wistful voice.

Jeff spared a glance away from the road, wondering what it was that he heard in her voice. He couldn't see her face since she was looking out of the window away from him.

He didn't understand her. That much was evident. He'd given her a hard time and she'd jumped on him with both feet, then ripped through his accounts like a tiger. The last thing he'd expected was for her to pronounce them sound and offer to loan him the money he needed.

If their positions had been reversed . . . he didn't think he would have been as understanding. He'd pushed his own fear and frustration off on her and she'd smiled and those green eyes had shot him down.

"Still snow in Pittsburgh?" he wondered, making conversation.

"A little." She looked back at him. "Mostly gray slush. It'll be spring there soon."

"Why'd you do it, Dana?" he asked quietly. "Why didn't you tell me to get lost and give somebody else that money?"

Branden had asked her a question that was similar when she'd gone home after their last encounter.

"I believe in your plan," she replied easily. "I think you can make this a viable business. With a little help."

"Why do you care?" he cornered her. "I mean, one way or another, the bank would find a way to make money. If not with my business then with someone else's."

"That's true," she admitted readily. "I guess I must just want you to do well."

He grinned at her. "My own beautiful, red-haired fairy godmother?"

Dana smiled back at him slowly and pushed a lock of hair behind her ear. "I, uh—"

The truck started making choking noises, then sputtered and died. Jeff let the momentum take them to the side of the road. Fortunately, there wasn't much traffic.

"What's wrong?" Dana asked, startled.

"I'm not sure," Jeff replied ruefully. "Slide over here, will you? Start the engine when I tell you."

Dana had been listening to those words all afternoon. "You seem to have a hard time with engines."

Jeff tossed her a dark look as he climbed out of the truck. "Pop the hood, huh?"

Dana glanced at her watch. It was nearly 5:40. If she wasn't at the airport in the next twenty minutes, she would be stuck there for the night.

"Try it." Jeff's voice came from behind the red truck hood.

Dana turned the key but there was no response.

Jeff yelled and pounded on something that she couldn't see.

"Try it again," he urged.

Dana turned the key and the engine came sluggishly to life, still chugging a little, but running just the same.

Jeff slammed the hood shut as Dana revved the engine to keep it going.

"I'll drive," she said as he started around.

"You don't know where you're going," he reminded her.

"The sign is right there," she told him, putting her foot down on the gas and wrenching the transmission into gear. "Just get in or I'll miss my plane."

Jeff jumped into the truck and Dana spun the wheels on the wet grass as she headed for the road.

He stared at her taut profile for a minute. "Does

your fiancé know what a terror you are?'' he wondered. ''Or are you keepin' it for the wedding?''

Dana shifted gears, grinding them slightly. ''My fiancé is none of your business.''

''Of course not,'' he agreed nonchalantly.

She made a quick left turn and a horn blared behind her.

''This must be city driving,'' Jeff conjectured.

Dana pressed the brake hard as they reached the front of the terminal. They both fell forward, then back against the seat.

''I'm glad it wasn't any farther.'' He breathed a sigh of relief.

She glared at him, surprised to see a ghost of a smile in those gray eyes. Was it possible he was joking with her, teasing her?

''I have to go.'' She opened her door and picked up her coat. ''Promise me that you'll take a minute every so often and either call or write and let me know what's going on.''

He nodded. ''I'm sorry if I played fast and loose with you, Dana. I won't let it happen again.''

''Thanks.'' She smiled, then glanced toward the front door. ''It'll be a miracle if I make this plane. Good-bye, Jeff. Keep me posted on the boat repairs.''

''Thanks!'' he yelled after her as she ran for the front doors. ''See you later.''

Dana slowed down as she entered the terminal.

The ticket counter was just inside the door and a smiling attendant assured her that there were plenty of seats left and that she had enough time to make the flight.

"Do you have your return ticket?" she asked, taking Dana's name.

Dana started to reply and take out her ticket when it hit her. She'd left her briefcase on the boat. Her wallet and return ticket were in it.

There was nothing else to do. The woman at the counter continued to smile as Dana thanked her and walked away. Watching the 6:00 P.M. to Pittsburgh taxi down the runway for takeoff, Dana dialed Branden's home number and left him a message.

"It's me, Branden. I'm going to be down here for another day. Things were just a little more confused than I expected, but I should be home tomorrow night. Sorry about dinner. Love you. 'Bye."

She went outside into the rapidly falling twilight, hoping to find another cab that could take her back to Wilmington.

Instead, she found Jeff Satterfield, leaning against the side of the truck, waiting.

"The truck won't start?" she wondered, amazed to find him there. She smiled despite herself.

He was amazed to see that shy little smile on her face. "Call it a hunch."

"A hunch?" she demanded.

"I knew you wouldn't be leaving yet."

She regarded him dubiously. ''I would have been on that plane . . .''

''Would have?'' he prompted, one eyebrow raised.

''But I forgot my briefcase at the boat.''

''Convenient,'' he drawled, opening the truck door for her.

She climbed in and he closed the door behind her, getting in on his own side, a smug look on his face.

''I had every intention of going home,'' she retorted a little breathlessly.

''You know what Freud said,'' he reminded her. ''Everything means something. Maybe you left your briefcase on the *Runner* so you couldn't leave tonight.''

She took a deep breath. ''Why would I do that?''

He started the engine, allowing her a quick glance. ''You tell me.''

''I don't—''

''Maybe,'' he filled in for her, ''you want to finish tackling my computer mess. Or maybe you knew I was going by the best place in the state for dinner on my way back to the docks.''

He paused at the parking gate to wait for the arm to lift after he'd paid the lot attendant. He looked at his unexpected guest and wondered why he hadn't seen that little hint of doubt in the curve of her smile. He thought he'd memorized everything about her, but he hadn't noticed that wishful, dreamy glow in those big green eyes.

"Or maybe you were hoping we'd get the *Runner* going in time for you to have a short ride out of the harbor."

"Or maybe I just forgot my briefcase," she fumed, suddenly feeling oddly vulnerable. "I already had dinner plans for tonight and I wouldn't push my luck with the boat any further. I was probably just lucky that I didn't get sick today."

"That may all be true," Jeff admitted after the parking gate lifted and he pulled out into traffic. "But sometimes it takes fate dressed up like an accident to show us what we're missing."

She sighed. "I suppose just getting my briefcase and dropping me off at a motel is out of the question?"

"I suppose so," he agreed with a laugh. "Dinner and a little small talk is all I ask, Dana."

"Do I have a choice?"

"Do your friends call you Danny?" he wondered, heading back through the traffic.

Dana felt a headache coming on. She closed her eyes and took a deep breath. Dinner. How bad could it be?

Chapter Three

Dana awakened the next morning with a start. Her head was pounding, and she felt queasy and disoriented.

How bad could it be? she'd wondered, trying not to feel the air hit her face like a sledgehammer. It could be pretty bad. The traveling, the rush, the stress—she'd been overcome with fatigue. Even coffee at dinner with Jeff couldn't keep her awake.

She couldn't recall where she was. She remembered dinner at the edge of the river and going back to the boat.

Too many late nights and early mornings. She groaned, sitting up slowly. She might not have crossed any time zones, but she had been exhausted.

She looked around herself with a jaundiced eye. Where was she?

The room looked familiar, but her foggy mind refused to place it. Then her glance landed on the computer in the corner and it all came back to her. She was on board the *Blockade Runner*.

She looked down at her crumpled suit and ruined stockings. She had no idea where to find her shoes. What had possessed her to sleep on the boat?

Fortunately, her patch still seemed to be working. She touched it gingerly behind her ear. At least she wasn't seasick.

She recalled coming on board the boat, but couldn't recall falling asleep. She did recall that the next flight out of Wilmington was 9:30 that morning. She scrambled to get her things together.

Well, in her mind, she was scrambling. In reality, there was a loose connection between her brain and her body.

It took a few minutes to swing her feet off the bunk and another few minutes to figure out where to put them.

The floor was a long way down. She was looking at it one moment and on it the next.

She crawled carefully under the edge of the bed she had been sleeping in and looked for her shoes, muttering under her breath when she couldn't find them. How could she have lost her shoes?

''Looking for something?'' Jeff asked, pausing in the doorway to admire the sleepy, tousled-haired woman presented to him. He decided that there was something to be said for gray suits after all.

He startled her and she hit her head on the bed frame.

''My shoes,'' she retorted, groaning.

''You threw them in the water last night,'' he said with a chuckle. ''You said they hurt your feet.''

She backed out from under the bed and stared up at him in horror from the floor. ''What?''

He shrugged, his arms folded across his broad chest. ''Remember? You said they hurt your feet and threw them into the—''

''I heard you the first time,'' she interrupted sternly, her head aching. She looked at her wrist and found that her watch was gone as well.

''I don't know what happened to that,'' he admitted, seeing the gesture.

''Do you know what time it is?'' she asked, exasperated.

''I never wear a watch,'' he responded, ''but I'd guess from the sun, sometime after noon.''

''After noon?'' she wailed, putting a hand to her head. ''I missed my plane again!''

''Looks like it.''

She started up from the floor, regretting the hasty movement when her head beat a rapid tattoo.

''Take it easy,'' he persuaded, helping her to her

feet, then taking her by the arm and guiding her to a chair. "I'll make something for that headache."

"I can't believe I did this," she remarked, holding her head in her hands. "I fell asleep on this boat. I missed my plane, and I threw my shoes in the river."

"Well, not exactly," he countered, running a hand uneasily around the back of his neck.

"Not exactly?" She moaned, not looking at him.

"Not exactly," he repeated. "You threw your shoes in the Atlantic. We were already at sea . . ."

"What?"

". . . by the time you threw your shoes overboard," he finished. "Don't you remember?"

"At sea?" She stared up at him as though he had just told her that she was in outer space.

What had seemed like a good idea the night before was suddenly taking on the aspects of a nightmare to Jeff. He crouched down beside her, looking into her stricken face.

"You said you really wanted to go out on a cruise. We got the engine running about midnight and you said you wanted to go out."

Dana was dumbfounded. She couldn't believe it. It had to be a trick. She would never—

"Let's go outside," she said very quietly. She did briefly remember confessing to a longing for an adventure, but . . .

He nodded. She was looking a little pale. She'd feel better on deck.

Dana plunged through the doorway and stumbled up the steps into the sunshine. The glare reflecting off the water made her shield her eyes. She stood in the middle of the deck and stared, turning slowly, as she realized that he had told the truth.

There was water everywhere. No sign of land. Little whitecaps furrowed the great expanse of gray-green meeting the sky at the horizon with its vivid blue. Fluffy white clouds danced above them.

They were at sea. There was nothing around them but miles of water.

Jeff took one look at her face then urged her into a deck chair. He ran down the stairs to the galley when he thought she would be all right until he got back.

He should have known better, he decided as he poured her a glass of orange juice and found two aspirins. Women were unpredictable.

He knew he hadn't been wrong about that wistful look in her eyes yesterday. He might have been wrong in thinking that she'd admit to it in the clear light of morning.

Something moved in the far corner as he was about to pick up the glass and head out on the deck. He raised a frying pan instead, thinking it was a wharf rat. He'd found them before on board. They could be a menace.

Penny's bright face emerged from beneath the tarp as he stood over her with the skillet in his hand.

"What are you doing here?" he demanded, putting down the frying pan.

"I thought you might need my help," the girl replied easily. "You know, pushing the witch into the oven or something."

"Penny, you're supposed to be in school."

"I know." She hung her head. "I wanted to come with you."

Jeff could only imagine the consequences. "Did you tell Mattie?"

"I left him a note," she returned quickly, watching his face to see if it was going to be all right.

"Well, we're going to be heading back anyway," he said with a short smile at her. "I guess we'll deal with it then."

"Great! I can make lunch," she volunteered.

"Good," he agreed, picking up the glass of orange juice. "I'm taking this topside for Dana—"

"Dana, is it?" She grinned and rolled her eyes.

"If you were a few years younger, I'd spank you," he admonished her. "That better be one heck of a lunch."

Dana was where he had left her. She was staring out at the water with an expression he could only classify as witless horror.

"Here." He put the glass into her hands. "Drink this and you'll feel better."

Dana didn't look at him, but she tried to drink the mixture in the glass. Suddenly a wave of seasickness overcame her. She ran to the side rail, gasping for fresh air.

"I can't believe it," she cried, clutching the rail for support. "I can't believe I'm in a boat at sea!"

"You insisted on paying for it with your Visa," he informed her proudly.

She turned to face him then and he noted that her color was better even though he began to see a buildup of temper in her eyes.

Redheads, he mused. *Can't live with them, can't toss them overboard.*

He recalled the night before when she'd unsteadily tried to cross the plank to reach the schooner. She'd wrapped her arms around his neck and sighed gratefully when he'd caught her swaying form close to him.

"You were going to fall," he'd explained when she'd looked up at him.

"And you saved me," she said and smiled sweetly. "Thank you, Captain."

This Dana didn't smile sweetly. She looked as though she wanted to rip his head off.

"You! This is all your fault!"

"Calm down, Danny." He tried to ease the friction between them.

"Don't call me that!" she demanded. Where had he picked up that name?

"You told me to call you Danny last night," he

answered her unspoken question. "You said you liked it better than Dana."

"I said you could call me that just to shut you up," she assured him.

"Shut me up?" He stood his ground as she advanced on him across the deck.

"You kept talking and trying to get me to talk to you and I was so tired. Then you tricked me into paying for a cruise—"

Jeff began to feel his own temper rising in turn. "I didn't make you eat dinner or tell me about your family. I didn't insist on you coming back to the *Runner*. You told me that you wanted to go on a cruise. Then you fell asleep in the cabin."

"Was this some kind of revenge? Or are you some sort of weird, perverted kidnapper?"

Jeff glared at her furiously. "I'd never be weird or perverted enough to kidnap *you!*"

Penny stuck her head out of the galley window. "Lunch anyone?"

Both adults turned to face her furiously and she quickly retreated.

But the interruption brought a brief space of clarity.

"I'm sorry," Dana relented, sinking back down in the deck chair. "I really didn't think you'd, well . . ." She glanced up at him. The sunshine made her teeth hurt.

"I'm sorry, too, Danny—Dana," he quickly

amended. "I thought you wanted to come out here. You went on about it all evening."

"Maybe I did." She sighed, forcing herself to look up at the blue sky and the sparkling water. "Doesn't everyone have moments of insanity?"

He grinned. "I know I do. I guess I thought everyone else did, too. That's why I brought you along."

"You thought it was my moment?" She looked at him, standing there next to her in the sunlight, and she had to smile.

There it was again. He shook his head dazedly. It was that smile that had put him in this mess. A little trembling, a little uncertain. It tugged at a soft spot he didn't know he had for ambitious overachievers.

"Lunch," he said finally. "Lunch will make us all feel better."

He was right, she decided an hour later. She did feel better, if that was possible being miles out at sea when everyone expected her to be in Pittsburgh. She sat in a sheltered corner of the schooner eating cheese chunks and wheat crackers and drinking mint tea.

"The mint tea is good for your stomach," Penny informed her.

"It's good," Dana commented, trying to calm down. What was done was done. Besides, it wasn't the girl's fault. "I appreciate the lunch."

"It's not much." Penny shrugged. "Most of the food stored on board is canned stuff. We can eat some of that for dinner tonight. Jeff usually stocks up fresh supplies when we go out on a long cruise. I guess he didn't expect to be out for very long this time."

"Dinner?" Dana pressed her, catching the single word. "Will we still be out here for dinner?"

"We're pretty far out, Ms. Eller," Penny apprised her of their situation. "It'll be midnight before we reach town even with a good stiff breeze."

"Call me Dana," she encouraged the girl. If she was going to be out there all night, she needed someone besides Penny's confusing, irascible brother to talk to on the trip.

She glanced up at where he sat drinking coffee and steering the boat. After their disagreement and lukewarm truce, he'd gone back and started the engine, saying something about the wind not being right for the sails. He didn't say another word to her.

"Thanks," Penny replied, then saw her line of vision. "He's not a bad guy, really."

"Really?" Dana turned back to her. She smiled at Penny. "I think it would be strange if you thought he was."

"I suppose." Penny shrugged. "He's always been great to me."

"How long have you lived with him?" Dana asked, knowing that she was prying, but telling Jeff Satterfield telepathically that he had only himself to blame.

"About two years. Our parents were killed in a car accident. Jeff gave up his job to take care of me."

"I'll bet all of this is really exciting," Dana ventured, wanting to make friends with the girl, if not her brother.

"It is for me," Penny agreed, and looked out at the water. "Jeff was captain of a cruise ship, but they wouldn't let me live with him. I didn't care once I saw the *Runner*."

Dana remembered from his résumé that he'd been a captain of Regal Cruise Lines. They had spoken very highly of him.

"So that's why he quit," she conjectured. She'd wondered from the start. After all, those jobs were well paid and secure. Running your own business was a risk at best.

Penny thought about it, squinting into the sunlight. "He said he didn't want me to have to go and live with Aunt Harriet. He was gone a lot when he was a cruise captain. He said he always wanted to own his own boat anyway, like Dad. He and Mattie and Dad always wanted to do just what they're doing."

Dana smiled at her. "Can't ask for more than that, can you?"

"If you'd like to change clothes and take a shower, I can show you where," Penny volunteered, beginning to like the witch.

"I'm afraid I didn't bring a change of clothes with

me,'' Dana said mournfully. Her suit had long since gone past serviceable.

''Come on,'' Penny urged. ''I think I can find something for you.''

Jeff finished his coffee, watching the two talking on deck. Penny's young face was animated and he could only guess at her conversation. Dana's head was copper bright in the sun as she sat on the deck, looking up at Penny.

He would have to remember to warn her about that, or by evening, she'd be toast. That milky white skin didn't lend itself well to the hot sun.

He should have known better, he reflected, looking out over the hull where it met the sea. Women were never who they seemed to be. Hadn't he learned that lesson the hard way?

''Jeff!'' Penny approached him, climbing over some rope. ''I'm looking for something for Dana to put on. Her suit is kinda hacked. I took her down for a shower, but all I could find is some of your clothes.''

''That's about all that's on board,'' he told her. ''It's only for a few hours. Give her some of my stuff. At least it's clean.''

''Okay. Jeff?''

''Yeah, Penny?''

''You aren't going to make her mad anymore, are you?'' She smiled at him. ''I sort of like her.''

"Sort of?" he wondered.

"Well," she confided, "she's a little uptight. She keeps worrying about what everybody's going to think. I told her what you always tell me. *She* knows the truth. That's all that matters."

"Sometimes," he replied, "it's not that easy, Penelope."

"Don't call me that!" she protested. "It makes me sound like an old lady."

"Well, that was our grandmother's name."

"I know. But Grandma Penelope wasn't old like some old people. You know?"

He grinned. "I know. You'd better go and get those clothes before our guest is finished in the shower."

"Is she?" Penny wondered, wrinkling her nose. "Is she our guest?"

"Like any other paying customer," he assured her, but didn't add that he would be giving this guest her money back at the end of the tour.

"Okay. I'll give her the royal treatment."

"Thanks, Penny. What would I do without you?"

"You'd be lost!" She shrugged and kissed his forehead. "I'll have our guest back on deck looking for treasure."

Jeff didn't bother to disabuse her that Dana Eller would hardly want to look for treasure with them. Getting back to the mainland was her only priority and with luck, the engine would hold up going top speed to do that as quickly as possible.

There had been a moment the evening before when Dana had looked at him with those big green eyes and he'd looked at her soft pink lips and . . .

Why did he always find women attractive who had absolutely nothing in common with him?

She had just tossed her shoes over the side and was grinning at him like the Cheshire cat. Her hair was a little windblown and her eyes sparkled in the moonlight.

He'd always known it, he decided. He was a bad judge of women.

Dana put Jeff firmly out of her thoughts and stepped into the shower. The hot water felt wonderful. Cleaning away the grime from the day before, it became simpler to clear away the cobwebs that had clouded her brain.

It did a great deal toward making her mistake more bearable. In the cold and sober light of day, she was willing to admit that she was at fault.

Maybe Jeff had encouraged her, but she remembered thinking those traitorous thoughts long before she'd confided them to him.

Hadn't she wanted to sail out of the harbor on that Brazilian ship? Wasn't that the sound of wistful thinking in her voice when she'd spoken to him?

Well, she'd had her fun. It wouldn't be easy explaining why she was so late getting home. Everyone would be worried and her grandfather would feel as though she had let him down. With him, it was always personal.

She had always worked hard at trying to please him. She sighed, picking up the clean white shirt Penny had left for her. It was demanding, trying to be what he wanted her to be. Sometimes, she wasn't sure if she lived her life to suit herself or him.

She loved him, of course. That was why she tried so hard to do what he expected. He had never asked for her loyalty. She had simply given it.

The shirt Penny had given her was obviously Jeff's. It smelled of fresh air and sunshine when she put it on and buttoned it. She wondered who washed his clothes and hung them out to dry. Nothing else smelled like sun-dried cotton.

It was too big, tentlike, but she rolled up the sleeves and tied the tails at her waist. The pants were a little more difficult. Jeff was at least a head taller. She had to roll the legs of the blue jeans up carefully or they fell back down.

The jeans were worn and soft, faded nearly to white, but they felt clean against her skin. She used her own belt to anchor them at her waist.

She smiled down at the shoes Penny had provided. They were impossible. She could have put both of her feet into one of them.

"Are you finished?" Penny asked, knocking on the door.

"I think so," Dana answered, opening it. "I think I'll have to go barefoot for the day."

"Sorry." Penny frowned. "Mine are too small."

"It's just for one day," Dana replied. "I'll be fine. Thanks for the clothes and the shower, Penny."

"No problem."

"So, can I get a cup of coffee like your brother had outside? I think I'm going to spend some more time with his computer since I'm here for the day anyway."

"Sure," Penny responded. "But I think you should spend the day in the sun instead of in the cabin. You're really pale."

Dana laughed. "I don't spend a lot of time outside. And it *has* been winter," she pointed out in fairness.

"That's true. You'd probably burn anyway."

"I burn like nobody believes," Dana agreed with her. "So I think the computer is my best bet."

Penny shrugged. "I'll get the coffee. Cream and sugar?"

Dana picked up her glasses from the bedside table. "Black, no sugar. Thanks, Penny."

Two hours went by while Penny laid on a deck chaise and read a magazine. Jeff yawned and rubbed a hand over his stubbly face. It had been a long night and he'd only grabbed a few hours' sleep. He was tired and he needed a shower.

There had been no other craft in the water for most of the afternoon. The sky was clear and the water was calm. He called Penny down from her place on the deck and gave her the helm.

"I'm going to take a shower and change clothes." He glanced surreptitiously around the deck. "Where's Ms. Eller?"

"Dana's working on the computer. She's been down there forever. I don't know what she thinks is so interesting on it."

"Dana, huh?" Jeff rolled his eyes at her and grinned. "I guess she's an accountant at heart."

Penny frowned. "She said she was afraid of getting sunburned, too. She is very pale."

"I know," he agreed. "Maybe I can help with that. You stay here. Yell if you need me."

"I know what to do," she told him. "I'm not a baby, you know."

He left her there and wandered down into the living quarters. There were three cabins on the *Runner*, one bath, and the galley. The computer was set up in the corner of the smallest cabin and that was where he found her.

"You should come topside for a while," he encouraged, sitting on a chair just behind her.

"Why doesn't this make sense?" she asked as she mangled a pencil in her mouth.

"I'm a terrible bookkeeper?" he suggested.

"But the figures . . . ah! Here it is!" The computer

screen flashed a row of numbers, then suddenly went blank.

"What happened?" she wondered, hitting the top of the monitor with her hand.

"That won't help," he informed her fatalistically. "The monitor just dies out from time to time. It'll come back up in a couple of hours."

"Oh." She frowned. "Is there another one?"

Jeff considered telling her that they always took a laptop for backup, but one look at her pale, tense face made him change his mind.

"That's it," he lied with a clear conscience. The woman might as well go home with a little tan at least. "Come up on the deck while the sun's still out."

"I burn," she told him plainly. "Who's steering the boat?"

"Penny has the helm. It practically takes care of itself. I just came down for a shower and a change of clothes."

Dana looked down at his clothes that she was wearing, her pale face turning a bright pink. "I hope I'm not—I mean—"

He smiled at her, though his eyes did a quick sweep of her in his clothes. "I don't need them right now. I have something else."

She let out a long breath. "Oh, thank you. I mean—"

Dana looked at him with the dark stubble on his

lean jawline and the smoky eyes that had so coolly assessed her. He looked as though he hadn't slept all night and when she thought about it, he probably hadn't.

"I'm sorry I accused you of . . . of coercing me into going on the boat."

"That's okay," he replied as though it happened every day. "But as long as you're here, you might as well catch some rays."

"I don't tan," she said quietly.

"No problem. I have something that will keep you from burning. At least you can sit in the sun for a while. Vitamin D is good for you."

"I'm afraid I don't just sit very well either," she ventured apologetically.

"Workaholic, huh?" he queried.

She nodded. "Maybe there's something I can do."

His mind wandered quickly. "I think I can arrange something."

Twenty minutes later, her face covered in sunblock, Dana was polishing the brass portholes on the deck.

"Is this the treatment guests usually have on the *Runner*?" Penny wondered, watching Dana with a cloth in one hand and the brass polish in the other.

"Guests who can't just sit in the sun," he told her with a smile.

"How'd you get her off the computer?"

"Waited until that old monitor went out like it always does, then refused to drag out the laptop."

Penny laughed. "You're a genius."

"Just a good host," he told her. "I'm going below to catch that shower and change. Watch her so she doesn't fall overboard."

"Maybe you should just tie a rope around her waist," Penny suggested.

He sighed. "I don't know where you got that mouth, young lady."

She grinned and stuck out her tongue. "Mom always said I got it from you, like all my other bad qualities."

There was a stifled screech and a loud splash that followed a short descent to the water.

"Tie a rope around her waist, huh?" Jeff speculated, taking off his deck shoes and grabbing a life preserver. "Sounds like a good idea."

Chapter Four

Dana was a good swimmer. She'd won awards for it when she was in school. But the icy water was a surprise. It took her breath away for a moment, long enough for her to become disoriented.

What she was really worried about was the massive hull of the *Runner* connecting with her head as it was propelled through the water. She tried to strike out away from the boat but felt herself pulled back by the wash as the craft proceeded.

The rush of water kept her from hearing the second splash. She only knew someone else was in the water when she felt an arm snake around her chest and felt a warm body beside her own.

The schooner had slowed to a stop in the water. Penny hadn't wasted any time in cutting the engine and letting down the anchor. She peered over the side, ready to throw another life preserver if it was needed.

"I'm all right," Dana tried to tell her savior, but the water kept splashing in her face. She gulped in cold salt water, then tried to pry the arm away from her.

"Don't panic," a voice close to her ear tried to reassure her. "I've got you."

"I can swim," she spluttered, but the hold didn't slack off. Like a wet rag doll, she was unceremoniously dragged out of the water and slung on the deck face first.

Large, rough hands began to move on her back, trying to make sure she hadn't swallowed too much water. She was flipped over urgently and a hand pushed her wet hair out of her face.

"I'm all right," she told him. "I'm breathing."

His dark wet hair was slicked back from his face. "Are you sure?" he asked, gray eyes laughing. "Mouth-to-mouth is my specialty."

"I'm fine. Really. Thank you."

"Blankets." Penny came to their sides holding two large wool blankets.

The sun was nearly down and the day had cooled off considerably. Dana felt her teeth begin to chatter and clamped her jaws down in a death grip.

"Here." Jeff took one of the blankets from his

sister and wrapped it around Dana. "You better get out of those wet clothes and into a hot shower."

"We might run out of clothes soon," Dana replied, then glanced up into his face.

Jeff looked at her, still holding the blanket closed under her chin. He bent down slightly and lifted her in his arms. "We better get you downstairs then, before anything else can happen."

"I can walk," she protested, wiggling her toes when they stuck out from under the blanket.

"Not on my deck." He shook his head. "Not without an escort."

Penny refolded the blanket she'd held for her brother and whistled a little as she followed the two adults down the stairs.

She made hot coffee and listened to the weather reports on the radio. There was a storm coming up, unusual for that time of year. Small craft warnings hadn't been issued by the Coast Guard, but everyone was keeping an eye on the front.

"Storm?" Jeff guessed, hearing the tail end of the report as he came into the galley. He had changed into the only thing dry, a pair of his oldest jeans. Dana had taken the last dry shirt.

"Maybe." She shrugged. "You look like those guys on the soap operas."

He ran his hand across his face. "I think I better get us back home before I worry about winning a beauty contest."

Dana walked into the galley wearing only a large blue shirt. It was big enough that it hung down to her knees. There wasn't anything indecent about it. But she felt funny standing there with them.

"Sorry about the swim," she attempted. "One minute I was polishing and the next the boat moved out from under me."

"You have to get used to it," he commented wryly. "I'm glad you weren't hurt."

"It was more a surprise than anything."

Penny laughed. "I'll bet. Coffee?"

"Please." Dana shivered. "I'll hang those wet things out on the deck so they can dry."

"No!" Brother and sister chimed in at once.

"Penny can take care of it," Jeff added. "We might run into some rough weather before we make the river."

Dana felt next to her ear for her patch. "Oh, no." She groaned. "It's gone."

"What?" Jeff asked, quickly searching over her for anything he noticed different.

"My seasickness patch. It must have come off in the water."

Penny and Jeff exchanged glances.

"I need to go topside and get us moving again," Jeff explained. "Penny, will you get Dana some gingersnaps?"

Dana sat in the darkened cabin as the boat began

to move, wondering when she would begin to feel that rolling in the pit of her stomach again.

"Here's the gingersnaps," Penny said, after knocking at the door. "Ginger is supposed to be good for seasickness."

"Thanks." Dana smiled at her. "How old are you, Penny?"

"Twelve. Thirteen in three months."

"You're very mature," Dana said, nibbling on a cookie. "When I was your age, I don't think I could do anything useful like piloting a boat."

"I kind of grew up on one boat or another," Penny recalled. "My dad was a riverboat pilot. He used to take me on the ships when he was working and let me look at their controls. They were complicated."

Dana looked at her, seeing the thin face and long neck. There was a sprinkling of freckles across her face and her eyes seemed enormous. "It sounds like your dad and you had a wonderful relationship. You must miss him a lot."

"I do," Penny agreed thoughtfully. "But Jeff has been great. I want to be a ship's captain when I grow up."

Penny looked up suddenly as the sound of the engine died. "That might be trouble. I better go up and see if Jeff needs a hand."

Dana closed her eyes and prayed. How much worse could it get?

She shouldn't have asked. The engine died and couldn't be revived. For some reason, there was no wind, so it was pointless to raise the sails.

She sat on her bunk and listened to Jeff as he worked on the engine. Tools clanked and there was intermittent shouting. Around midnight, she put on a pair of still-damp jeans and crept up on deck.

Penny was asleep at the helm, waiting for her brother's word to try the engine again. She was curled into a tight ball, shivering on the deck. Dana awakened her enough to lead her below to her cabin and pulled a blanket up over her.

She took her place on deck, locating what she hoped was the starter switch and sat and waited for Jeff to call out again.

The night was very still around her. She didn't think she had ever seen such darkness. It was as though they had been swallowed whole and she could step off the boat into nothing. The water was black and calm, barely making the boat move.

The stars were bright beneath sometimes fitful clouds. She looked up and knew there had to be a moon out since she recalled one from the night before, but the best they got was a luminous cloud that covered the light.

"Try it, honey," Jeff called out from below.

Dana hoped she was doing the right thing. She pushed a red switch. The engine made a noise, but didn't turn over.

She heard a thud, followed by the sound of heavy footsteps coming up to the deck.

"That's all I can do," Jeff told her, surprising her when he suddenly laid down flat on the deck. "My back is killing me. They don't make those engine compartments for people over two feet tall."

The small running lights picked out his form lying still on the shiny wooden surface.

"We'll have to hope we can put up the sails and catch enough breeze to get to the nearest island before the storm hits in a few hours."

"Can we outrun a storm?" Dana asked calmly.

Jeff turned over and sat up. "I didn't see you. Where's Penny?"

"I made her go to bed for a while. She was exhausted," she explained.

Jeff looked at her darkly. "Thanks. She thinks she can do it all."

"She's not the only one," Dana was quick to point out.

"Meaning?"

"When did you sleep last? You must have been awake most of last night. You've been awake all day. Maybe you should try to get some rest until the wind comes up."

"It's only about three hours till daybreak," he said, yawning. "The storm should send some wind our way before the rain. We'll have to get the sails up in a hurry and catch that first part of the front."

Dana watched him lie back down on the deck and saw him staring up at the sky, his hands folded across his chest.

"I'm sorry I got us into this mess. I thought the engine was in good shape or I wouldn't have taken her so far out."

She laid her head back against a coil of rope and tried to relax. "It's been an adventure."

"At least you aren't sick," he noted with relief, thinking how much worse that could be.

"I'm not," she agreed, surprised not to have thought about it for a while. "Maybe I'm waiting for the storm."

"Some people adjust after a while," he told her. "Some never do. If you do adjust, even a bad storm won't affect you."

"If you don't adjust, even a pier makes you sick," she finished.

He laughed, a rich sound in the darkness. "A pier, huh?"

She chuckled. "If it moves."

"You'd think they would have hired someone with a stronger stomach at a marine bank."

"They didn't have much choice," she replied quietly, watching the stars move in and out of the clouds. "My grandfather is the chairman. Someday, that's probably what I'll do, too."

"You don't sound very sure about it," he remarked.

"As sure as I am about breathing." She sighed heavily. "Someday, when everyone else retires, I'll be sitting in that big office, making all those decisions."

"Okay," he amended. "You're sure about it. But you don't sound happy about it."

"Happy?"

"When I was working for Regal, everyone thought that was all I could possibly want. It was good money. People respected me. I had a hundred crewmen at my beck and call twenty-four hours a day."

"Not to mention women in bikinis throwing themselves at you," she added. "I've seen the commercials."

Jeff smiled at the idea. "The reality is a little different. But it was a good career."

Dana yawned. "It does sound like something that would make most people happy."

"But I was never home. When Mom and Dad died, things had to change. Penny needed me to be there for her. But I can't say that I miss the cruise line," he explained.

"So you quit your job, came back home, and started your own business," she reflected.

"Only after two years of fighting with everyone else in the family about who should raise Penny and saving every nickel to buy the boat. I finally got a break on the *Runner* from a friend in Portsmouth."

"That's amazing. I'm afraid to have goldfish,"
she concluded, realizing, not for the first time, how
much more there was to people than their loan ap-
plications. "Maybe that's why you have to be more
courageous than I am to follow your dream. Sometimes, it asks too much of you."

He gazed up at the stars and shook his head. "I
don't think it's so much courage as desperation. I
don't know how to be someone else. I had to be there
for Penny."

Dana thought about her grandfather briefly. "I
know how that can be. Sometimes, it's just easier to
do what's expected of you."

"Well," Jeff added for the sake of argument, "if
you don't want to be bank chairman, which sounds
like a pretty cushy job to me, want do you want to
be?"

"It's not that I don't want to be bank chairman,"
she replied, feeling uncomfortably disloyal to her
grandfather even talking about it.

"That's what it sounded like to me," he responded lightly. "Come on, Dana. Just between me
and the moon, if you could do anything you ever
wanted to do, what would it be?"

A few random images flew across Dana's eyes. "I
like to build things," she whispered.

"It's only us out here in the middle of miles of
water, Dana." He put his hands under his head and
tried to imagine what she looked like as she said

those words. "What kind of things do you like to build?"

"Shelves, tables." She sighed, as though admitting a deadly sin. "I rebuilt my grandmother's china cabinet into a sewing hutch."

"And no one knows, do they?" he guessed.

"No one knows," she admitted softly. "I rent a little building, a—a storage unit. Last year, I bought a lathe."

"Dana Eller, master craftsperson." He smiled up into the black sky. "I like the sound of that. Why not?"

"Because Dana Eller is a bank officer in the line of my grandfather, my father, my brother, and my uncle. My grandfather has been working with me to take his place since I was sixteen. I could never disappoint him."

"Even if it doesn't make you happy?"

"There's more than one way to be happy," she responded. "I do a good job. I help people do things with their lives."

"But not yourself?"

She didn't answer. She closed her eyes against the bright points of light in the sky.

Dana was dreaming. In her dream, she was standing on a pirate ship, a beautiful lacquered table next to her. Jeff Satterfield, in typical black pirate garb, was standing beside her, admiring the table.

"You made this, didn't you?" he asked, smiling raffishly at her.

Her grandfather, father, mother, brother, and Branden were all being held away from her by the rest of the pirate crew.

"Tell him you didn't do it," her grandfather urged. "Tell him you're a banking Eller, like the rest of the family, Dana. Tell him!"

"All right," she said, then yelled loudly, "All right!"

She sat up on the *Blockade Runner*'s deck, wondering what she had been yelling about. The boat seemed to be tilting oddly around her and she looked out at the beginning front of the storm around them. The sky was leaden above the boat that was being tossed roughly in angry, white-capped gray seas.

It was the most frightening sight she had ever seen. How would they survive a storm in the middle of the Atlantic in a sailboat?

Jeff was in a yellow poncho, scrambling to release the sails. His dark hair was dry and blowing wildly about his face.

"Good morning," he hailed her from the foremast. "Looks like we're in for a rough trip."

"What can I do to help?" she asked quickly, her own hair, for once, refusing to stay in place.

"Go below and help Penny."

"You can't mean to sail this all by yourself?"

"Do you know anything at all about sailing?" he questioned.

She shook her head. "No. Not a thing, but . . ."

"Trust me, Dana. I need to know that you and Penny are safe below. It's going to be all I can do to handle getting us into a harbor somewhere. I don't want to wonder if we're all on board."

Dana glared up at him mutinously. "I think there must be something—"

"Keep Penny below. I know she knows a lot about sailing, but I don't want to take a chance that she might lose her footing when it starts to rain."

Jeff watched her go below, sorry that he had to insist, but worried about the weather. It was going to be a tough job getting through the heavy seas. The *Runner* wasn't a small craft, but high winds, rain, and rough seas weren't ideal sailing conditions.

He'd tried the engine once more, but there had been no response. He was going to have to go home the old-fashioned way, tacking like crazy and hoping to stay one step ahead of the storm.

Penny smiled when she saw Dana's face but realized at once that she had been banished from the deck as well.

"He can't do this alone," Penny told her. "He needs another pair of hands up there."

Dana sat down beside her on the bunk with a sigh. "I don't think it's going to be you, Penny. He was pretty sure about that."

"Why not?" the girl demanded.

"Because he's worried about losing you," Dana told her. "Has he eaten?"

"I don't think so," Penny replied with a worried frown between her eyes. "I was up while the two of you were still flaked out on the deck. He never came down here."

Dana remembered their conversation before she'd closed her eyes in the darkness last night.

Master craftsperson, she mused, smiling.

"Well, why don't we make him something to eat and some coffee? Then we'll work on the rest of it as it comes up. Okay?"

"Okay," Penny agreed.

They walked into the galley together and started dragging out canned food. It was no mean feat managing to cook as the boat dipped and bounced across the waves.

"So, do you think we're near one of these islands?" Dana wondered, bringing the girl's attention to a map posted on the wall.

"Jeff says we're near old Stump Island. There's nothin' there anymore. Just an old abandoned lighthouse and an old church and cemetery. But there's a good harbor there to get past the storm."

"Where is that?" Dana asked, studying the map.

Penny smiled at her as though she were a child.

"Well, it's not on the map, exactly. No one goes

there. That's the tourist map. We use it for treasure hunting on the tours.''

''Treasure hunting?''

Penny picked up her subject enthusiastically. ''Well, you know about Blackbeard, probably, but what a lot of people don't know is that a pirate named John Abbott took some stuff from him and hid it away, then tried to escape. He was killed, of course. Nobody stole from Blackbeard. Sometimes ships would hide their cargo from the pirates by burying it on an island and sailing back for it later when there wasn't a pirate ship behind them.''

''But sometimes, they didn't make it back? Like poor John Abbott?'' Dana guessed, looking at the map. ''What are these round red marks?''

''Places where people have dug for treasure before and couldn't find any. Sometimes, you only find a few things. Dad found a carved smoking pipe that's in the maritime museum at home. They said it dates back to the 1700s.''

''That's exciting,'' Dana admitted. ''Any treasure on Stump Island?''

''Might be.'' Penny shrugged. ''People have looked there, but I don't think they've ever found anything.''

They cooked breakfast as they talked, putting the oatmeal in bowls and the coffee in plastic mugs with sip tops.

''I guess you should take this out to him,'' Penny

told her dourly. "If I go up on deck, he'll strangle me."

Dana laughed. "But you're willing to risk my life?"

"What's the worst he can do to you?" Penny demanded with a quick smile. "He can ground me until I'm eighteen. I'd never get to date or drive or—"

"Okay, okay," Dana gave in gracefully. "It sounds like it's starting to rain. Is there another poncho? I don't think I should get this shirt wet. I might be wearing it a few more weeks."

"In the closet." Penny pointed. "I'll listen to the weather while you're topside. Are you any good at cards?"

"No." Dana frowned, thinking of the disastrous games she'd lost to her brother.

Penny laughed. "Good! We'll play when you get back. Maybe I can beat you. I always lose to Jeff."

"Thanks."

Dana pulled on a yellow poncho like the one Jeff was wearing and pushed her way up the stairs to the deck.

Conditions had worsened while she'd been below. The boat was rocking inside, but it was far more frightening facing the wild elements out in the open. The waves looked large enough to swallow the boat but the hull stayed afloat, dipping and dancing with the white foam.

"Watch it!" Jeff warned before he moved a sail in front of her. "Didn't I tell you to stay below?"

His face was wet with rain. The poncho had done little to keep his head dry. His eyes were the color of the sea around them and his mouth was a worried line.

"I was elected to bring you coffee and oatmeal because I can't be grounded," she explained. "You have to keep up your strength. You can't get us home if you pass out and fall overboard." She looked at the turbulent water around them. "And I'm not crazy enough to jump in after you in that water."

He looked into her face, seeing the real fear in her bright eyes, thinking how different she looked standing there in his clothes with her face wet and her hair a mess.

Which Dana was the real woman? He could imagine her in jeans with her lathe and dirty hands, but she was bound to follow her grandfather's dictates of gray wool and perfect composure.

"All right," he gave in. "Just to make you feel better. You'll have to stay up here and hold the wheel while I eat."

She swallowed hard, looking at the waves that towered above them. "All right."

"Don't worry," he said, moving away from the wheel as she put her hand on it. "The *Runner* has been through worse. This is a small storm for the Atlantic. The big ones don't come in until fall."

"I don't want to see one bigger than this," she told him plainly. "My family might have a history of seagoing, but I don't."

"At least you aren't sick," he reminded her, taking the coffee and oatmeal from her as she put her other hand on the wheel.

"I don't know why," she replied, her voice husky with fear. "What do I do?"

"Relax," he said. "You aren't steering a car through heavy traffic. Just hold it where it is. It'll be okay."

She did as she was told, gripping the wheel until her knuckles turned white.

"Relax," he said again, this time from just behind her. He put the coffee cup upright in his poncho pocket and put the bowl in a small indentation in the deck to hold it.

Dana felt his arms come around her, his wet hands slipping over the top of hers on the wheel. He tickled her fingers until she laid them lightly on the wheel under his.

"This is one of the best-built schooners in the world. She could weather a hurricane," he whispered near her ear.

The wind whipped around them and the sea surged against the side and deck of the boat, but they stayed on course.

"I hope she doesn't have to," Dana replied

breathily, feeling her heart rate and pulse rise dramatically with his nearness.

She could feel the comforting warmth where he stood against her back. His arms reached around her easily and his head could have rested on top of hers.

''That's better,'' he encouraged, not making a move to eat his breakfast, enjoying the feel of her next to him. ''The *Runner* is a lady. She needs to be coaxed, not mauled.''

Dana took a shallow breath, feeling herself treading in dangerous waters that had nothing to do with the storm around them. ''How close do you think we are from shore?''

''Not far now,'' he replied. ''The island has a sheltered, deep harbor leeward that should protect us from the storm. I appreciate you keeping Penny company. I know she thinks she has to be with me on everything, but it means a lot to me to know that she's safe.''

The rain slanted back against them with a broad gust of wind.

''I guess I better eat this and let you get back below,'' he observed, moving away from her and picking up his bowl and spoon.

Dana recalled all those old movies where the captain stood on deck with his feet planted slightly apart, holding the wheel firmly even as the ship was going down. She looked out at the big waves as the schooner went up and down the mountains of gray water.

"The ships in the movies looked much bigger," she said randomly. "And some of them didn't make it."

"We're probably not going to hit any icebergs out here," Jeff replied sarcastically. "Think of it as man, or in this case, woman, against nature. Holding her own, daring the elements."

"Watching the fish swim in and out of her ears." She groaned.

He laughed, then narrowed his eyes against the rain and the mist. "Look! That way, doubting Thomas." He directed her face with a light touch. "I think that's dry land."

"Not in this storm," she quipped, still holding the wheel.

He smirked down at her. "Very funny. Okay, just land then. I would think you'd be happy to see either right now."

"I would," she agreed. "I am. What do we do now?"

"We start taking in the sails," he replied. "Think you can hold the wheel without falling overboard? Or do I need to tie you to a mast?"

She pushed back her hood to look at him. "That was an accident. I wasn't expecting the boat to move like that. Go and do what you have to do. I'll be fine."

She watched him, careful to hold the wheel the way he showed her. The bright yellow of his poncho was clearly visible, even with the waves crashing over them and the heavy rain beating down on them.

One of the sails was tied securely to the mast when a large wave pushed the boat up, then tilted it as it came over the bow.

One minute, Jeff's yellow poncho was there on the rain-soaked deck. The next it was gone. ''Jeff!'' Dana felt her heart skip a beat. What should she do?

Chapter Five

""P enny!'' she yelled, hoping the girl was close enough to hear.

"Dana!" she yelled back. "Where is he?"

"I don't know! Come up here and hold the wheel!"

Penny slipped and slid across the deck. The schooner was in the island's harbor. The waves were already noticeably smaller and the wind wasn't quite as strong.

"Should we drop anchor?" Penny wondered as she grabbed Dana and held on to her with trembling hands.

Dana had no idea, but it sounded like a good suggestion. "Let's do that, then you hold on to the wheel while I see if I can find out what happened to your brother.''

''The *Runner* might drag the anchor until we get those sails down,'' Penny warned.

Dana looked up at the towering sails left unfurled against the dark sky. ''Okay. Okay.'' She tried to think of what the correct procedure would be in a case of someone being overboard.

Penny, though she had more experience, was obviously too worried about her brother to think clearly. Dana shrugged as she realized that she would have to make the decision. It was a clear case of a rock or a hard place.

''Okay. Drop the anchor and we'll take that chance until we can find out what happened to Jeff.''

She left the girl at the helm and struggled across the deck, holding on to whatever came to her hand.

Jeff was not on deck. Dana wished she could dial 911 and someone would come and take care of the problem. What should she do? Jumping overboard didn't seem to be the answer. How would she find him in the midst of the heavy waves?

Terrible thoughts of him drowning while she dawdled made her look over the side of the boat, holding the rail for dear life.

''Jeff!'' she yelled when she saw his yellow poncho dangling at the end of a long rope.

He lifted his head, the hood pulled away from his face, his hair soaking wet. ''Pull in the sails!'' he yelled back at her between mouthfuls of salty water. "Pull in the sails!"

Dana scrambled to do what he instructed. She slid to the closest mast and fought her way through the thick canvas to find the cords to lower and tie down the sails. She didn't know if it was the right way to tie them down but it was the best she could do.

"The sails are dragging the anchor!" Penny screamed at her. "Did you see him?"

"He's holding on!" Dana shouted back, trying to be heard above the roar of the storm.

The main mast was huge when she stood at the bottom of it and the sail looked like miles of wet canvas that flapped in the wind and refused to come down. Her fingers aching with the rain and the chill, Dana gritted her teeth and pulled at the sail. She could only hope that she didn't damage it and ruin their only chance to get back to Wilmington.

But for the moment, stopping the forward motion of the schooner was the most important thing. At that moment, all she could think was that she wished she had a big knife to cut them down!

The cords wrapped around her hands and tangled at her feet, but she managed to get the huge sail down. She wrapped and rewrapped the sail to the mast until she felt certain it wouldn't come free.

It was amazing the stupid things you thought at times like that, she considered.

As she ran across the deck to the side of the schooner to try to help Jeff back on deck, she looked up at the island and thought she saw a light. A big, round bright light.

Of course, there couldn't have been a light, since Penny had told her that no one had lived on the island in fifty years.

It was probably panic and stress, she decided when she looked back again and there wasn't anything but the rain-soaked dark strip of land in the distance. It was terrible what fear could do to the mind.

She reached the edge of the deck as a hand was reaching over the rail, followed at once by a bright swath of yellow vinyl.

Penny skidded to a stop next to her and together they each grabbed an arm and helped Jeff back on deck.

Dana saw that he had managed not to be swept out to sea by grabbing a line as he went over the rail. He had clung to the side with it in his hands until the boat had stopped moving.

Jeff dropped the line and she could see that blisters had already formed on his palms and fingers.

"I guess we're going to have to make sure you have an escort from now on," she told him, frighteningly glad to see his dark face and smoky eyes.

"Isn't this where you pick me up and take me below?" he wondered, wiping a wet hand across his face.

Dana lifted one of his arms while Penny took the

other so that he could lean on them as they walked across the deck. She looked up at him then, his black eyelashes, spiky with water, fringing the sea-deep depths of his soul.

"This is as good as it gets," she informed him, then stared intensely into his face. "Don't ever do that again! You scared us to death!"

She was close enough that all he would have had to do was lean his head and touch her lips. The wind seemed to have quieted around them and the boat was not rocking as fiercely.

"Are you all right, Jeff?" Penny asked from his other side.

"Yeah." He nodded, looking from wet face to wet face. "Let's go below."

Stump Island was only a mile wide, barely visible from the schooner in the heavy weather. Peering through the rain and the waves, it didn't look big enough to protect them from the storm.

But the harbor was protected by its U shape that curled around itself, cocooning them from the worst of the storm. Sailors for a generation had taken shelter there before trying to approach the mainland. The "Graveyard of the Atlantic" was no place to be if there was any doubt about safety.

The island had no docking facilities. They would have to take a small rubber raft to reach the shore. Jeff shot down that idea before Penny could finish explaining it to Dana.

"So, we're staying on board for the rest of the storm?" Dana gulped and resisted the urge to put one hand on the wall for support.

Jeff grinned down at her, toweling his hair dry. He'd taken a hot shower and managed to find a pair of mostly dry jeans. "That's it. We'll wait it out here. It's safer than trying to make it to shore. I'm not sure there's anything on the island that has a secure roof, anyway. With this wind and rain, any of those old structures could come down around our ears. No one's done any upkeep here for a long time."

The three of them started out in the galley at the small table, playing poker. Dana quickly saw that she was outmatched by both brother and sister and conceded her toothpicks to them both.

"I think we should play something else," she suggested as the hours dragged by and she lost at dominoes and dice. "Something I can win."

The wind howled like phantoms around them and the rain slashed against the deck, but the boat swayed peacefully at her anchor as though ignoring the bad weather.

Jeff glanced at Penny. "Do we have any banking games?"

"I don't think so," she said with a twinkle in her eye. "Unless we play Monopoly and we let her be the banker."

"That sounds like an unfair advantage," he said seriously.

Dana glared at him with a slow smile dawning on her face. "And the two of you spending hours learning to cheat at poker isn't an unfair advantage?"

"Isn't there something in the rules of the sea that allows a captain to throw someone overboard when they question his honesty?" he asked Penny while never taking his eyes from Dana's gaze.

"Oh, for the good old days of plank walking." Penny sighed and they all laughed. "I'm hungry anyway. Let's eat."

They ate a meal of canned macaroni and cheese, Penny and Dana complaining out loud about the quality of the food. Jeff threatened to lock them both in their cabins with only bread and water.

Penny hooted with laughter. "We don't have any bread!"

"Yeah." Dana held her spoon full of macaroni and cheese up and watched it plop back down to the plate. "I think this is torture enough."

They argued about football and talked about trivia through the meal. Penny brought out candles to conserve power and the already dim afternoon took on the look of late evening.

Jeff went into his own cabin after lunch to use the radio, trying to let the mainland know that they were all right.

The storm was making communication impossible.

He'd radioed back to Mattie to let him know that
Penny was with them before the front had moved in,
and Mattie had let him know that someone had
called, looking for Dana.

"He sounded like he thought you kidnapped her."
Mattie had chuckled, repeating the conversation he'd
had earlier with Dana's fiancé. "I think the man with
the big ring will come after her."

Jeff had frowned, but the situation was impossible.
"We'll be back as soon as the wind picks up or the
engine's working."

Nothing had really changed but he knew Mattie
would be worried about them being out in the storm.
He tried to get through again, but there was no reply.
He had no choice but to wait and let them know they
were okay after the storm passed.

He sat staring at the radio for a long time after
he'd switched it off, listening to the wind and trying
to form a picture in his mind of the man who was
going to marry Dana.

He'd be very proper and hardworking, he decided,
playing with the pens on the desk. Someone who
wore a suit well and played tennis regularly. Probably a banker or an accountant.

What was it that women loved about accountants
anyway? he wondered crossly. Was that what Dana
was looking for? Someone who always wore a three-
piece suit and never got his hands messy?

He looked down at his own hands, callused and

rope-burned, and sighed. He had his father's hands. Working hands. His mother had loved his father. They'd been married forty-two years. But maybe she had been looking for someone different, or maybe the clothes didn't matter to her.

He didn't know what it was, but he knew Dana was out of his league, despite her secret dreams of making furniture. She would marry her banker/accountant and she would forget she had ever made a sewing hutch out of her grandmother's china cabinet.

Shaking himself out of those thoughts—the weather was depressing enough—he went in search of his two companions.

Dana and Penny had retired to Dana's cabin and when Jeff heard them giggling, he knocked on the door.

"Come on in," Penny called, laughing.

They were sitting cross-legged on the bunk, Dana's entire array of makeup spread between them.

"Oh, great!" Jeff laughed. "I always wanted to go to a girls' slumber party."

"Sit down," Penny invited. "We can give you a makeover, too."

"I don't think so, thanks," he declined, but did take a chair to watch.

Dana was finishing Penny's eyes, carefully applying eyeliner and mascara.

"You don't really need this," she told the girl.

"You've got great dark lashes anyway. I have these scrawny red lashes that no one can see."

Penny giggled. "How do I look?" She batted her eyelashes.

"Too old," her brother complained.

Penny and Dana giggled and rolled their eyes.

"I'm going to grab a Coke," Jeff decided, not wanting to know what came next.

He stayed in the galley, watching the storm from the porthole for a long time.

While Penny and Dana giggled in the cabin, he put on a poncho and went topside to check if there had been any damage to the boat. The wind was still whipping the water into a frenzy, but the storm was easier to handle in the harbor.

Rain was heavy enough that he couldn't make out more than a sliver of the darker land a few hundred yards from their anchor, but it was enough that he knew that it was there.

The storm tumbled his emotions.

He thought about holding Dana in his arms; the smell of her skin and the way she looked at him when she told him not to fall overboard again. He hated to admit it, even to himself, but he couldn't stop thinking about her.

He had to be crazy to be attracted to her. Worse than crazy. At least relationships he'd had before had been with women who'd grown up in the same area, with the same background.

Dana Eller was a whole different story. They had nothing in common, except for a kiss, and that at a precarious time. She would fly back to Pittsburgh as fast as the first jet could take her when they got back to the mainland.

But he couldn't deny that she felt good in his arms or that her lips had felt soft as velvet beneath his. Those green eyes and that sweet smile were enough to make him forget everything. Even the huge engagement ring on her finger.

He would do better concentrating on getting them back, he decided, shifting his stance uncomfortably, and forgetting those thoughts.

He took one last look at the storm, then went back below. Dana and Penny were still giggling in the cabin, but he knocked and joined them again. It wasn't a good time to be alone.

Penny was returning the favor, putting makeup on Dana. Dana's eyes were dramatically darkened and Penny was in the act of outlining her lips with a pencil when he walked into the cabin.

Jeff watched while Penny concentrated hard on getting just the right outline, then began to smooth on the rich color.

Dana's gaze flew to his self-consciously, but she couldn't speak and she dared not move or risk a line of red going halfway across her face. She held her lips parted, just a little, while Penny carefully blended the lipstick on her mouth.

Jeff's eyes narrowed on the silent invitation she presented with her upturned face and parted lips. The cabin had become a little warm and a little smaller than was comfortable. Yet he couldn't take his eyes from the color slowly moving across the gentle curve of her lips. . . .

"Okay, blot!" Penny told her quickly, handing her a tissue with a giggle.

Dana took a deep breath and managed to look away from Jeff's intense gaze. Her own heart was pounding and the color on her cheeks owed nothing to peach blush.

"Doesn't she look great?" Penny asked, turning to question him.

Penny had swept Dana's hair up on her head, securing it with a barrette they'd dug out of her cosmetic bag.

"You both look beautiful," he complimented wisely when he was able to get past the choked feeling that had threatened to keep him from breathing. "Let's take a turn on the deck, shall we?"

Penny eyed him as though he were a pariah. "You must be kidding! We're not going out in that weather and ruining our look. Get with the program, Jeff."

The adults exchanged glances over the almost-teenager's head and Jeff groaned, leaving them alone again.

"Men just don't get it, do they?" Penny asked her newfound friend.

Penny has a lot to learn! Dana considered with a wry smile. "Sometimes they don't understand."

"What about this man, Dana?" Penny asked, holding up her ring hand so that the light caught on the large, sparkling diamond. "Does he understand?"

Dana thought about her question as they both looked at the ring. "Branden is wonderful. We both know the same people; we like the same things. We both expect the same things from our relationship."

"Does that mean that you love him?" Penny wondered, captivated by the ring.

"Of course," Dana intoned flatly. "We've been engaged for three years and now that his job is more settled, we'll probably get married."

Penny smiled wistfully up at her. "I wish Jeff could meet somebody great like you."

"What about you?"

"I'm too young to get married!" She put out her fingers and counted on them. "I still have to finish high school and go to college before Jeff will even let me look at a man."

Dana smiled. "I suppose so."

Penny shrugged thin shoulders beneath her Death By Terror T-shirt. "It's okay. I'll find someone to love someday."

"That's what's important."

The day dragged on, Penny and Jeff talking Dana into a game of Monopoly. They were hard-pressed to keep the money and the pieces on the game board, and Jeff cheated outrageously to Penny's constant laughter.

"You can't decide to put on a house as I land on your property!"

"I'm the landlord," he reminded her, piling on three little green houses. "I can do anything!"

"I'm never renting anything from you," Penny declared.

"Wait until I'm the banker." He glanced at Dana and smiled fiendishly. "I'm going to take everything!"

"Bankers aren't so bad," Dana felt compelled to defend.

"Of course, they're not," he agreed. "As long as they get what they want."

"If people who did business with the bankers were more dependable and responsible . . ."

"Okay, you two!" Penny called a halt to the feud. "We're trying to play a game here."

They ate canned spaghetti for dinner and Penny sighed, pushing hers around on her plate.

"I hope the storm clears tomorrow. I don't think I can stand another day of this stuff."

Dana agreed. "If this is what you feed your paying tours," she said disparagingly, "they'd better think about bringing their own food."

Jeff ate his spaghetti and reached for Penny's

plate. ''I love this stuff. What are you guys talking about?''

Penny laughed. ''It was all those rich meals when he was a cruise ship captain,'' she assured Dana. ''They spoiled him for real food.''

Dana laughed and started to take another bite of her food. The wind outside sounded stronger and the waves, even in the closed harbor, seemed to be getting larger.

She put the spoon down and worried the napkin with her fingernail. She knew her family would be concerned, especially when they heard about the storm. What would they think?

Penny and Jeff saw the worried frown between Dana's brows and exchanged glances across the table.

''It's going to be okay, Dana,'' Penny said quietly.

Jeff nodded. ''The storm is supposed to break sometime during the night. Once that happens, we're just a few hours from home.''

Dana smiled at them. Both brother and sister's faces were turned to her with familial earnestness etched into their features.

''One more game of Monopoly?'' she suggested bravely.

It was only 8:00 P.M. on her watch when they decided to call it a night and went to their separate cabins. The day had started out dark and had never achieved normal daylight quality. It was as dark at 8:00 P.M. as it had been at noon.

The full force of the storm still shoved at the schooner. No one mentioned going topside before the lights were turned out and they settled in for the night.

The motion of the boat wasn't making her sick, but it was difficult to get comfortable in the bunk when she felt constantly tossed from side to side. The idea of sleeping when her eyes were wide open and she was expecting to drown any moment wasn't a pleasant one either.

She lay on the bed, eyes wide open, staring into the darkness. Finally, when she couldn't take the constant shifting any longer, she got up and sat in the chair against the wall.

Feeling a little lost, she thought about when she was a child and had a bad dream. Her old nurse would pick her up and sit in the rocker with her, singing and telling her stories until the feeling passed.

It would have been nice if there was something that simple that could distract her from the storm that was crashing around her.

She thought about Jeff's arms around her, about the strange stirring she felt when he was near her. Just his looking at her, as Penny had put on her lipstick, had sent her reeling.

What was she thinking? She was wearing Branden's ring on her finger. She had heard of people who went away from home and lost all sense of themselves, but she wasn't one of them.

There was a soft rap at the door and Jeff whispered her name.

Dana swallowed hard and tried to remember that her life was centered and focused. She knew who she was and that was all that mattered.

"Dana," he said again as he walked into her cabin. "I'm sorry. I didn't think to talk to you about sleeping through this."

"What?" she asked, clearing her throat.

"When I take people out who've never been at sea, I always talk to them about the best way to sleep."

"I'm not really tired," she replied, hoping he would just go away.

"Great," he decided. "Me either. How about some chess?"

"I don't know . . ."

"Afraid you can't beat my strategy?" He aimed for her pride.

She held up her chin. "I've been playing since I was six. I was the chess champion in college."

He nodded. "I'll get the board."

Dana won the first game, then lost her concentration and her queen on the second. Jeff kept looking at her. She could feel his gaze on her. It was distracting.

"Winner takes all," Jeff said as they set up for the third game.

"What are we playing for?" she wondered idly, hoping to distract him.

He considered her question. "Let's say a truthful answer to a difficult question with each piece. Agreed?"

She looked at him, wondering what he was thinking. She knew she could beat him if she could maintain her concentration.

"All right."

Jeff had the first move. His knee brushed against hers and she made a clumsy second overture.

"Okay," he pursued, taking her first piece. "What's your fiancé's name?"

Dana frowned at him. "Branden Williams. I'll even throw in that he works at the bank."

She could see the pattern to his game when she lost her next piece. When he made his move, his long fingers accidentally came into contact with hers.

"Next question." He caught her gaze. "When are you getting married?"

"I'm not sure," she sputtered, starting to get angry. "You're cheating, Jeff."

"How?" he queried innocently.

Dana wanted to answer, but what would she say? *When you touch me, I can't think? When you look at me, my brain turns to mush?*

Instead, she decided that two could play his game.

When it was time for him to make his move, Dana gently nudged his foot with her toe.

Jeff glanced up at her and he faltered. Dana took his pawn.

"My turn," she said in a self-satisfied tone. "Is there someone serious in your life?"

Jeff's eyes narrowed on her triumphant green regard. "No, I haven't been lucky enough to find anyone who could put up with me."

Warming to the game, Dana commented on being thirsty. "I'll get you a Coke," he volunteered after she'd taken his next piece.

"No, that's okay," she told him, smiling when she got what she wanted. "Why did you bring me out on this cruise?"

His gaze swept over her with the force of the storm outside the schooner. "Because you asked me to."

"You felt sorry for me," she stated, seeing it in his eyes.

"Only one question per piece," he retorted, fixing his gaze back on the board.

Dana tucked a stray lock of hair behind her ear and concentrated on winning.

"Where'd you get that?" he asked vaguely a few moves later. They had both managed to keep their pieces safe from the other.

"What?" she asked without thinking, looking up from the board at his face.

"That." He reached across the small table space

between them and his fingers touched her collarbone next to the silver locket around her neck.

"That wasn't fair," she replied breathlessly when his fingers didn't move and instead stroked over the satin-smooth finish of the silver. "You weren't supposed to ask a question until it was your turn."

"Sorry." His hand dropped away, but the damage was done. Dana lost another pawn and her bishop to him.

"That was cheating," she repeated, still feeling warm from his touch.

"Touching you?" he queried in a deep voice. "You touched me."

"Ask your questions," she responded, trying to gain control over her rapid pulse.

He reached across again and her face turned up to him in question as his fingers closed on the locket. "Where did you say you got this?"

"My father," she whispered in a husky voice. "When I turned eighteen."

"It looks like an antique," he observed, feeling her pulse against the back of his fingers as he held the locket. It was beating as fast and irregular as his own.

"It is," she agreed. "It belonged to my great-great aunt Rose. Her husband was a merchant sailing captain. She, uh . . . waited for him to come home for twenty-two years."

"And did he?" Jeff questioned softly.

Dana felt the light caress at the base of her throat, but its pull went down through her spine, making her legs feel weak.

"Yes," she whispered, lost in his eyes as she spoke to him. "Even though everyone else said that he wouldn't, she waited and he came back. He gave her this locket."

Jeff felt himself being drawn closer to her, to the silk of her skin and the curve of her lips.

Dana felt his warm breath on her mouth and her lips tingled, parting slightly, issuing an undeniable invitation.

Chapter Six

"It's getting late," Jeff murmured, then moved away from her. The gleam from the overhead light had caught on her engagement ring, bringing him back to his senses, reminding him of reality.

What was he doing? he wondered, stowing away the chess pieces and the board.

Dana watched him closely from beneath the fall of her hair. Had she wanted him to kiss her? she asked herself. Had she wanted to feel his mouth on hers again, without an apology for mistaking her for someone else?

"Good night, Dana." He started out the cabin door.

The storm buffeted the schooner. Dana knew she

wouldn't be able to sleep and he would leave her alone in the darkness again.

"Uh, weren't you going to tell me something about sleeping during the storm?"

Jeff looked at her, knowing that he ought to leave. She was really getting to him.

"Please," she added, a little desperate for just a few more minutes of his time before she was alone to wait for the morning.

He felt a wave of lonely longing wash over him and he closed his eyes for an instant, trying to get a grip.

"Okay. I'll show you what I mean," he relented. "And then when you do want to sleep, it'll be easier."

"Okay," she agreed.

He switched off the light and stood for an instant in the darkness. "You'll have to lie down on your bunk."

"Oh!" she managed to say, feeling his nearness as he stood there while she went and lay down on the bunk, holding tightly to the side of the bed, hoping she wouldn't roll on the floor at his feet.

"Your head needs to be this way for starters." He slipped an arm under her shoulders, her hair caressing his bare skin. He moved her efficiently from one side of the bed to the other, telling himself to take a deep breath.

"That's much better," she lied, gulping.

He laughed. "That's not the secret by itself. You have to move with the natural rhythm of the boat. The water rocks one way, but you're fighting it."

"I, uh—"

"Just relax," he invited, his voice potent magic in her ear.

"You tell me that a lot, but I'm not really a tense person. I—"

"Shh. Part of relaxing is not talking."

"Oh."

"Now you cross your feet at the ankles," he instructed, moving her foot across the other, "on your back. And put your hands on your stomach. Your body will move but it'll sway with the boat instead of against it."

He leaned over her as he guided her restructuring. He could smell the rain in her hair and hear the beating of her heart.

"Better?" he asked, his voice black velvet in the darkness.

"Much, uh, much better," she answered, reaching out a quick hand that connected with his hard chest as a gust of wind struck the boat.

"You have to relax to move with the boat," he told her. Her hand felt like a hot iron against him.

"I was trying," she said, a catch in her voice.

"We're not going to drown." He brought the subject out into the open.

She collapsed against him, hiding her face in her hands against his chest. "I've never been so scared in my whole life."

He felt her tremble with fear. He drew her close to him, enfolding her in his arms.

"It's okay. This is a bad storm. You've never been at sea before. Of course you're scared. I'm scared, and I live out here."

"But we're going to be all right, aren't we?" she pleaded for the knowledge. "You'd tell me if you thought we were going to go under, wouldn't you?"

"I'd tell you," he returned truthfully, trying not to smile at her sudden trust in his judgment. "But we're going to be fine. I could tell you stories about other storms that would make your eyelashes dark."

"Tell me." She scooted over toward the wall, giving him room. "Talk to me."

He put his legs up on the bunk, carefully sliding beside her, not letting go of her as he moved.

"Okay," he agreed, wondering who it was that had sent this woman to torment him. "The first time I went out with my father—he was a river pilot—a big gale blew up from the south. There weren't advance weather predictions so much back then. Everybody had to rely on what Dad used to call his nose for the weather."

Dana listened to him, the reverberation of his deep voice against her ear where she leaned against his chest. She could hear the beating of his heart in the stillness. He smelled of rain and fresh air and his hand stroked the skin on the back of her neck as he talked.

He was warm and close beside her. She closed her eyes and snuggled against him.

Jeff's voice cracked a little when she moved closer to him. He hoped that she wouldn't notice. She was warm and soft and fit very nicely next to him. Her head nestled in the hollow of his neck and her hand inched across his waist.

She sighed and he stopped speaking, the rain and the wind filling in the gap where his words left off.

"Why did you stop?" she wondered, enjoying the sound of his voice.

"I can't go on . . . like this," he admitted, feeling a roaring tide within him that equaled the wildness outside.

"Why not?"

He looked down at her, moving his head back only an inch from her own. "Because I don't want to talk with you this close."

"I, uh—"

"That's exactly what I mean," he murmured, closing the scant distance between them with his lips.

Dana closed her eyes and let herself lean into him. Her hand slid up around his neck, bringing him closer. The storm had ceased to exist; the swaying of the boat was just a tantalizing rhythm between them that brought them together.

Jeff felt as though he were drowning when he kissed her. It was that memory that had haunted him for the last year. It was that feeling that had made him look into her green eyes and bring her out on the *Runner*, even though the sane part of him told him not to leave the harbor.

There might not be anything right about them being together, but he couldn't resist her. They might not have anything in common, but he didn't care. It was that need that had fueled his anger against her. In her arms, he was willing to admit that he probably hadn't returned her calls or letters simply to see if she'd come back to him.

"Jeff." Dana sighed his name, realizing only when she felt his lips on her that she was still being kissed.

"You smell like spring." He teased her ear with his kisses. "And you taste like rain."

"I—I can't do this," she whispered, running her hand through his hair. "I can't cheat Branden this way."

Jeff was still at the mention of the other man's name. An image of the big diamond popped into his brain.

"Branden," he replied softly. "Engagement ring Branden?"

"We've been engaged for three years," she explained.

Jeff shifted so that she was by his side, her head on his shoulder.

"This might seem like an odd question, Dana, but are you in love with Branden?"

Dana considered her words as well as her feelings. "I've known Branden for five years. We go to the same parties; we're friends with the same people—"

"You go to all the right galleries together and you attend the same charity balls," Jeff finished impatiently. "That's not what I'm asking, Dana. Do you *love* him?"

"We're very comfortable together," she defended. "Now that we're going to be more stationary, we'll probably get married."

"Why does this sound like when you told me that you were going to be the bank chairman?" he wondered, sliding his fingers through the silk of her hair.

"It's not the same," she answered, quivering at his touch. "I'm not engaged to Branden because it's the right thing for me to do."

"Then you're engaged to him because you love him?"

"Yes," she said firmly. "I love Branden."

He sighed. "And you're kissing me because you're scared."

"That's right," she agreed quickly. "And I needed a distraction. Like . . . like my old nurse used to tell me stories when I had a bad dream."

Jeff shifted again so that he could see her face, his eyes intent on her in the pale glow of the safety light.

"Dana, I'm not your old nurse," he began, touching his lips to a spot near her temple. "And if you believe"—he kissed her cheekbone—"that you're not attracted to me"—he kissed a spot near her mouth—"then you're lying to yourself, sweetheart."

She told herself that she would have protested, but at that moment, he kissed her mouth, and the fierce longing that consumed her made her wrap her arms around him even tighter.

A torrent of emotion that she hadn't known existed until that moment when he'd kissed her last year, made her forget everything. There was nothing safe or right about it. There was nothing that could have prepared her for its devastating onslaught.

She'd tried to tell herself that he was annoying. That she thought about him because he was a monster and they didn't get along. But the reality was in his touch. She couldn't think when he kissed her and she couldn't pretend to be anything but enthralled.

"Dana." Jeff whispered, wondering if it was possible to get enough of her.

She looked up at him with eyes full of longing and lips tingling from his kisses.

He would have gathered her in his arms again, but the cabin door squeaked and he heard a small voice call his name.

"Oh, great!" Penny observed, opening the door

all the way. "You guys have already thought about being together. You could have told me."

She jumped into the bunk with them and pulled up part of the blanket on her body.

"All right. So are we telling scary stories or is Jeff telling you stories about other terrible storms where he was almost killed?" she wondered, looking innocently from one adult to the other.

"Terrible storms," Dana managed to say, bringing herself away from Jeff's embrace.

"Where I was almost killed," Jeff finished, clearing his throat. "Where was I?"

Dana laughed, feeling like a teenager. "You were telling me about your dad."

"Oh, yeah." Jeff laughed, understanding what had made her smile. "My dad and his nose for storms."

"Why are you laughing?" Penny asked, puzzled. "Is that some kind of adult joke?"

Dana dissolved into more laughter and Jeff followed her while Penny sat back, annoyed. And they said kids laughed at weird stuff!

Sometime during the long night, they all managed to drift off to sleep. When Dana first opened her eyes in the morning, it was to see a gorgeous beam of sunlight piercing the porthole. Dancing rainbows shimmered across the floor from the small crystal that was hung above her bed.

The storm had passed. The wind was calm and the

sky was blue. The water was a little choppy, but in comparison, it was smooth sailing.

She and Penny were a tangle of arms, legs, and blanket. She sorted them out carefully, trying not to awaken the sleeping girl. Penny looked very young and fragile with her dark hair splayed out on the pillow and her freckled face relaxed.

In the bright light of day, it was difficult for Dana to believe that she had been so carried away by Jeff's kisses.

She washed her face and looked in the mirror above the sink, touching her lips with a wondering finger, looking for any sign of the emotionally storm-tossed woman who'd taken her place last night.

Did she look a little wild-eyed and a little too . . . happy?

What was it about Jeff Satterfield that made her feel things so strongly? Anger, frustration, attraction, and exhilaration. She had ridden a carousel of emotions since she'd met him.

There was no doubting that something about the man drove her crazy. It seemed she was destined to either kill him or kiss him!

The logical part of her, the part that she was afraid she'd lost sometime during the long night, knew that it would be a mistake to believe there was anything between them.

She had been scared. Maybe he had been worried. She rationalized the moments they had spent together before Penny's timely entrance. It had been a comfort thing. Not a romantic thing, she decided, finishing her analysis.

She went in search of Jeff when she heard noises coming from below. He was working on the engine again.

"Any luck?" she asked, kneeling beside the hole in the floor that led to the engine compartment.

"Maybe." He looked up at her with grease on his face and a smile that lit up his eyes. "Try starting it and we'll see."

Dana went quickly up the stairs to the deck. There was debris across the shiny wood surface—seaweed, leaves, and sand. She picked her way through the storms's leftovers and tried the starter switch.

The engine didn't start, but it did make a noise that sounded promising. She waited and tried it again when Jeff called to her, and this time, the engine turned over. The schooner throbbed with the sudden sound after the silence.

"We got it!" Jeff joined her on deck.

"Are we leaving?" she asked.

"I'll have to go over the hull and make sure everything is seaworthy before we head out again. I'd rather call for a tow from the mainland than risk the deep water," he explained. "It should be okay now. You can turn it off."

Dana looked at him dubiously. "Wasn't that what happened last time?"

"If it is," he informed her brightly, "we can sail back. This is a sailboat."

Penny joined them on deck, delighted to hear that everything was working and that the storm had passed. "Let's eat lunch on the island," she suggested.

"Dana wants to make for home as soon as I'm sure we're seaworthy."

Penny looked at her in disbelief. "You don't want to see the old lighthouse and the chapel?"

Dana could tell by the look on her face that Penny was disappointed. It was only a few hours. She was so late already that it couldn't make much difference.

"I do want to see the old chapel and the lighthouse," Dana told her. She might as well, she considered. When would she ever be that way again?

They spent most of the morning cleaning up the boat. Penny checked the sails and corrected what Dana had done in haste the day before. Jeff put on a mask and flippers and swam around the underside of the hull to look for damage. Dana cleaned up the deck and polished the brass, careful of her footing.

The sun was warm overhead by the time the work was done. Jeff had called the mainland. They were all right and would be starting back after they visited the island.

Mattie had acknowledged and warned Jeff that Dana Eller's family was waiting for them.

Jeff nodded. "Did you tell them what happened when they called?"

"Called?" Mattie laughed. "They got down here last night, the whole kit and caboodle of 'em. Including her fiancé. They're standing outside the door right now, threatening to haul you off for kidnapping."

"Thanks for telling me," Jeff acknowledged. "We'll be back sometime today. When I know about what time, I'll let you know."

"Okay," Mattie answered back. "I'll try to keep everything together here until you get back."

Jeff finished the call and shrugged the threats aside. They could all think what they liked. He had nothing to lose. His time with Dana had been worth whatever they wanted to throw at him.

Dana sat on deck with Penny, waiting for him to finish. They talked about the coming summer when she was hoping to go out on tours every week with her brother. She told Dana about the boy she "sort of liked" who sat behind her in English.

"He's got these cool dimples," Penny confessed. "And blond hair."

"And he wears it kind of shaggy like a surfer," Jeff finished when he returned on deck to hear their conversation.

"Jeff!" Penny complained. "You're not supposed to listen in on other people's conversations."

"If we're going to go to the island, we better get

going. Mattie says Dana's family is really hot about her being out here with us,'' he replied with a frown.

"Does that mean we can't go?" Penny asked, glancing at Dana.

Dana shrugged. "I don't think another hour or so is going to make that much difference."

Penny was quiet, obviously in a thoughtful mood, while they lowered the raft and put the picnic basket into it, then headed for shore.

Jeff tried to draw her into a conversation several times as he rowed the raft through the water, but the girl didn't have anything to say to him.

"So," Dana finally said, deciding that not saying anything wasn't making it better for the pair with her, "why are the chapel and the lighthouse abandoned? It looks to me like we could have used a lighthouse yesterday."

"About a hundred years ago, there was an outbreak of smallpox on this island. It was a thriving little port and the village was a trading point for the islands around here. Then everyone died off," Jeff described briefly.

"Everyone didn't just die off," Penny corrected her brother. "People lived here for another fifty years. But no one would come back here to start over after the smallpox, so the people who stayed slowly died off."

"Then there was only old Jack left," Jeff added in a deep voice.

"Old Jack?" Dana continued, hoping to keep them talking. Anything was better than the silence.

"He was the lighthouse keeper," Penny told her, forgetting her wayward thought as she warmed to her story. "The strange thing was that when they found him dead, he was still in the lighthouse. He'd been dead for a while, but people had seen the lighthouse come on every night even after they thought that he had died."

"A ghostly lighthouse." Dana smiled. "That's pretty scary."

"The really scary part is that sometimes, people still see the light from the lighthouse. Even though there's nobody living here anymore."

The wind fluttered lightly over their heads and a gull wheeled and cried above the rapidly approaching shore.

Penny looked at Dana with her enormous blue eyes and Dana felt a chill move up her spine.

"You know yesterday? When we were trying to stop the boat and get your brother back on board, I thought I saw . . . something."

"Something?" Jeff questioned, one brow lifted as he looked in her direction.

Dana nodded. "A bright, round light. Off in that direction." She pointed where she thought it would have been yesterday.

They looked up toward the high hill overlooking the harbor and at that moment, the old lighthouse was visible, the sun beating down on its weathered frame.

''Cool!'' Penny whispered, staring at the tower.

Dana shivered again. ''I'm glad I didn't know about it last night.''

''Me, too.'' Penny shivered with her despite the heat of the sun.

They pulled the raft to the shore through knee-deep water that was chilly but tolerable. Little crabs scuttled away from their feet, hiding in the washed-up debris from the storm.

Penny picked up a stick and showed Dana the jellyfish that had washed up as well. Its glistening, strangely shaped body was drying in the sun.

''Can't we put it back?'' Dana asked as Penny moved it with the stick.

''They're dead,'' Jeff told her after tying the raft securely to a tree root. ''They can't be out of the water this long.''

''We could take it with us,'' Penny said cheerfully.

''No, we couldn't,'' Jeff corrected that notion. ''Remember last summer when you sneaked those jellyfish on board and forgot them? I didn't think we'd ever get the smell out.''

''He's such a baby about things sometimes,'' Penny whispered confidentially to Dana.

They followed the old track into the abandoned village. There were still about twenty houses, in various states of decay, that lined the dirt main street where weeds and nesting turtles had taken up residence.

They peeked into the doors and windows of the houses and the tavern. It was an eerie feeling, as though the people who'd lived there had stepped out but were coming back. There were still pieces of dusty old linens at some of the broken windows. A few of the tables in the tavern had glasses on them, thick with dust and sand.

"I'd like to go in and scavenge," Penny told Dana brightly, winking and nodding toward her brother.

"But the structures aren't safe." Jeff reacted instantly after having heard the request many times. "Someday, they'll probably knock all these old places down and build condos."

Penny rolled her eyes at Dana as if to say, "I knew he'd say that." "I'm going ahead to the old chapel."

"But not inside, right?" he inquired.

"I'll wait outside," Penny said dully. She raced ahead of them on the sandy path.

"Sorry about Penny. She gets a little moody sometimes," he told Dana when Penny was out of hearing.

"That's okay. It can't be easy for her," she responded, looking ahead of them at the tall grass and white sand.

"Penny and I are good friends most of the time. She handled our parents' deaths better than I did."

He paused. "I know that isn't what she's really feeling, though."

"She's a wonderful girl," she replied.

"That's the truth."

There was an awkward silence between them as they walked slowly up the path.

"Penny told me that she wishes that you could find someone and be happy, the way your parents were happy."

Jeff frowned. "I know. She's set me up with every unmarried waitress, mothers of her friends, and truck drivers, from here to Charleston."

Dana laughed lightly. "That must be awkward."

He looked at her intently. "I'm surprised she hasn't tried to set me up with you."

Dana felt the wind tug at her hair and the sand grit between her toes. "Is this where you say something about the sea being your only true love?" she suggested with a smile

He swept an encompassing look over her animated features and bright green eyes. "The sea is where I work."

He picked up a shiny, flat stone and skipped it across the sand. "I don't think everyone is destined to be as lucky in love as my parents were, though."

Penny came into sight as they crested the hill where the old chapel was situated. The trees around the chapel had been blown by the strong sea breezes for so long, their gnarled limbs looked as though someone had purposely poised them in a southern direction.

Tall grass grew around the stone chapel. Expensive lead-paned windows looked out over the rocky coastline with a magnificent view of the harbor. In the front of the church was a stained-glass window, still intact, that showed the resurrection scene in vivid detail. The effect on that deserted island amidst the ruins of other people's lives was breathtaking.

"It's hard to believe someone hasn't come to restore the chapel or at least claim that window," Dana said as they walked around the rough-hewn stone perimeter.

Jeff explained that the pews inside were all hand-carved from oak trees on the island. Wonderful scrollwork of saints and crosses had been wrought into every piece of work, making the house of worship a richly dedicated piece of art itself.

"It's really something, isn't it?" Penny said as they walked beside each other.

"The work that went into every piece of wood," Dana said admiringly. "It must have taken years to do all this without modern crafting tools."

"The strange part is how no one has desecrated anything. All of it is still intact. Just waiting for the wind and the tide to take it," Jeff murmured.

"The cemetery's this way." Penny led her away from the chapel to the far slope of the hill.

About a hundred graves were in the cemetery.

Some with headstones toppled over, some with no markers except rocks with initials carved into them. Moss was growing on most of them, obscuring their owners' final tribute.

''Everyone's buried up here, except old Jack,'' Penny told Dana, shading her eyes from the sunlight with one hand. ''He's buried at the lighthouse. They figured that was where he wanted to be.''

Dana thought about that bright light that had looked like a giant flashlight beam shining through the storm. She shivered as they skirted the cemetery and walked back toward the lighthouse.

Chapter Seven

They took the path from the chapel back to the coast of Stump Island, not more than a mile's hike over the sandy terrain.

The lighthouse was obscured by the high hill that made up most of the island. Built on a jutting promontory to better reach out into the night and to the sailors it protected, it was small in comparison with the more modern lighthouses.

It was barely taller than the chapel bell tower, possibly twenty or thirty feet. The top of the structure, where the light had been housed, had been destroyed. A rail ran along a catwalk where old Jack had once followed his nightly routines, but there were gaps in the wooden planking. The darkened windows stared out vacantly toward the harbor.

Heavy surfs and high winds had taken their toll on the aging structure. It wasn't hard to imagine that it wouldn't stand for much longer.

Dana touched the few remaining specks of white paint at the base of the structure and gazed up at the tower from the doorway that had once led up to the light. The door was open, barely hanging on rusted hinges that creaked with the slightest breeze.

She paused thoughtfully. It was a waste that the old lighthouse had been left to ruin. What did old Jack think about that?

Penny helped her brother spread a red-and-green checked blanket on the mostly sandy slope and laid out their picnic feast at the side of the lighthouse. Grass grew fitfully in the face of the strong sea winds and too-quick rain runoff.

"We couldn't be out here during high tide," Jeff informed Dana. "You can see where the tide line is." He pointed to the marks at the base of the lighthouse.

"Old Jack's grave is being taken, too," Penny pronounced sadly, seeing the small white cross in the line of erosion.

"That's probably the way he would've wanted to go," Jeff said, understanding the old man's love of the sea and the people who made their life on it.

"Like you and Dad?" Penny smiled up at him, her blue eyes full of love.

"Just like us," he agreed, touching her cheek with

a gentle hand, ''when I'm a hundred and ten. And even then, people will see me sailing the *Runner* out of the harbor at midnight.''

''Still trying to pay off your loan, no doubt,'' Dana teased.

Jeff laughed and Penny grinned broadly.

''You're okay for a banker,'' she told Dana.

''I'll take that as a compliment. Although where I come from, people like bankers and think highly of them.''

''You mean the other people of your family who are also bankers?'' Jeff remarked.

Dana laughed. ''Exactly.''

They ate lunch on the hillside and Dana felt at peace with the tumbling winds and the salt air. The gulls came down and looked for scraps of food. They threw them the remnants of their meal and Dana marveled at the birds.

''It's amazing how they know to come for the food after no one's lived here for so long.''

Penny looked at Jeff and they both burst into laughter.

Dana frowned. ''What's so funny?''

''The gulls don't just stay in one place,'' Penny explained. ''These gulls fly everywhere from here to Myrtle Beach and back again. If you threw that bird with the one black-tipped wing part of your lunch in Wilmington, he could be here for supper tonight.''

"I guess I'm not a bird expert," Dana admitted stiffly, getting up from her place on the ground.

"And you're not much of a card player," Penny conceded with a sad shake of her head.

"And not much of a sailor," Jeff joined in, starting to pack up the remains of lunch.

"But you're a really good sport," Penny backtracked.

"And you polish brass better than me," Jeff added with a wicked grin.

"Stop!" she pleaded. "I'm blushing!"

Penny linked her arm through Dana's. "We like you, Dana. Don't we, Jeff?"

Jeff linked his arm through her other arm, the picnic basket in his opposite hand. "I think we could get used to having you around."

"What do you say?" Penny asked.

"What are you asking?" Dana wondered as they started down the hill toward the beach where the schooner rocked at her anchor.

"We're looking for a good accountant," Penny said.

"The hours are bad and the money is lousy," Jeff admitted.

"But you could go for free rides on the *Runner*," Penny promised brightly.

"And we'd let you polish all the brass you wanted." Jeff grinned.

"And you could marry Jeff and be my wicked stepsister!"

"Penny!" Jeff warned.

Penny smiled at them both, then let go of Dana's arm. "Race you down to the bottom!"

"She loves to do that," Jeff said as they followed at a more sedate pace than the girl running through the tall grass.

"Run down the hill?" Dana inquired politely, feeling a little lost for words. Was it that obvious that she and Jeff . . . that they . . .

"No, embarrass me," he concluded. "It was only a matter of time. I told you she throws me at every unmarried woman we meet."

"I thought she understood that I was engaged," Dana replied nonchalantly, though her heart was beating quickly. It was the exertion, she explained to herself.

"She does understand," Jeff asserted quietly. "She probably just wants to make sure you're not marrying the wrong man."

Dana looked straight ahead, not daring to look him in the eyes. "I'm marrying the right man. She doesn't have to worry about it. Branden and I will make a wonderful team."

Jeff picked a blade of tall grass as they followed the narrow path down to the shoreline. "Penny's been through a lot. I guess she's a little sensitive."

"I'm going to marry the right person," Dana pressed forward.

"For the wrong reasons?" he wondered.

Dana shook her head. "Better the right person for the wrong reason than the wrong person for the right reason!"

Jeff stopped as they reached the sandy bank that separated the sloping hill from the shoreline. "There's always the chance of being with the right person for the right reason," he paused, looking directly at her.

Dana couldn't look away from that intent gaze. "And the chance of being with the wrong person for the wrong reason." She watched the wind caress his hair and squelched a wish that she could do the same. "What are you trying to say?"

He didn't answer at first, but slowly leaned forward, until his mouth was a scant breath from her own.

Dana felt the wind on her cheek. She could hear the sounds of the water and the birds, but she couldn't move and didn't dare breathe.

He kissed her. She knew that he was going to and yet she didn't move, didn't protest, even though she told herself that everything that had happened between them was a mistake.

His lips were firm and warm as they slanted across hers in a fierce hunger that made her feel a deep melancholy and loss.

She realized that he was saying good-bye.

"We'll never know, will we?" he questioned as he moved away from her.

When she could open her eyes, he was already over the dune and on the beach with Penny, loading the basket into the raft.

Dana was deeply moved by the emotions he'd raised in her. She wiped a tear from her eye and followed him to the raft.

Both adults were silent as Jeff took the oars, refusing Dana's offer to row them back out. Penny looked from one to the other, wondering what had gone wrong, then launched into a steady patter about school and MTV that remained with them until they reached the schooner.

They stowed away the raft and weighed anchor, Penny and Jeff moving in perfect harmony with the boat, doing all the work.

Dana looked back at the island, thinking about what Jeff had said to her, as well as the strange fate of Stump Island's inhabitants. Her eyes followed the silhouette of the lighthouse to the steep crest of the hill whose valley sheltered the little chapel.

At the peak was a cross etched into the brown rock with what looked like a dark spot in the center of it.

She called Penny's attention to it and the girl followed her gaze back toward the island.

"I've been coming here since I was a kid," Penny said in awe, "and I never noticed that before."

"What are you two looking at so intently?" Jeff asked from the helm.

"A cross carved in the rock," Penny replied, pointing. "Look!"

They all looked back, but the angle that the schooner had taken had caused a shadow from a cloud to fall against the hillside.

"I don't see anything." He shaded his eyes against the sun, but there was still nothing but the brown rock.

"Wait a minute!" Penny whooped, rushing below and coming back rapidly clutching a piece of paper. "Look at this! It could be the place where John Abbott hid the treasure he stole from Blackbeard!"

There was a mention of a cross marking a place the unfortunate pirate thief had hidden his stash. The map Penny held was full of places and markings where treasure had been found and where some people had speculated other treasure would be found.

"The island was settled for a long time after that, Penny," her brother told her kindly. "If there was a cross there, it was probably a marking for seamen to know there was a chapel on the island."

"We could go back and check it out," Penny pleaded earnestly.

"We'll be lucky to get back tonight as we stand, Penny," Jeff said flatly. "We'll have to come back after everything is settled."

"Settled?" Penny wrinkled her nose, looking at her brother.

Jeff glanced at Dana, then back at his sister. "We're all in plenty of trouble for being out here. You've missed school. Dana's got some people down here looking for her. We have to go back now, Penny."

"Okay," she agreed with reluctance, knowing she had no choice. "But we'll come back, right?"

"Right." Jeff smiled and nodded. *Just as soon as I get out of jail for kidnapping and we manage to buy another boat,* he considered thoughtfully.

The engine had worked fine getting them out of the natural harbor, but with the wind blowing steadily, Jeff had opted for the sails to get them home quickly.

"We'll be sailing across the wind," he nodded, eyes narrowed on the horizon. "We'll make good time."

Penny explained to Dana that sailing across the wind was the best way to sail. "It's faster and doesn't take as much work as it did last night."

The ocean was as calm that afternoon as it had been furious the day before. Sparkling sunlight danced in its depths. Schools of silvery fish trailed the schooner, leaping and twirling in their liquid world.

Dana sat on deck with some of Jeff's special sunblock protecting her skin, watching from a careful vantage point as he sailed the *Blockade Runner* home.

It felt as though they had been gone for a month. She was worried about what her family was going to say. For any of them to have come after her was amazing.

Technically, it had been a series of accidents and unforeseen circumstances that had kept them away for so long. Surely, they didn't blame anyone, as Jeff had hinted, for the unfortunate events.

She looked back across the deck at him, wondering why he hadn't told her before they'd left for the island.

He wore a black T-shirt that left most of his tanned, muscled arms bare, and tight, faded blue jeans.

If the sea captains of old had looked that way, standing on deck with their feet planted apart, the wind playing with their dark hair, she could well understand how women waited lifetimes for their men to return from the sea.

She thought about her great-great-aunt Rose who'd waited a lifetime for her husband to return from his voyage to Spain.

Everyone said that Rose had always believed that her husband would come back. She never let anyone convince her that he was dead. And like Ulysses's Penelope, Rose had remained faithful.

Afer twenty-two years, great-great-uncle Stewart

had returned to his bride and brought her the silver filigree locket from Spain that she wore until the day she died.

A lesson in patience, her father had told her when he'd given it to her.

"Everything is worth waiting for," he'd told her as he clasped the chain on her neck.

Dana didn't know if she had the perseverence of her great-great-aunt Rose, but if great-great-uncle Stewart had looked like Jeff Satterfield and had kissed her to distraction, calming her and intriguing her with his presence . . . she could understand why she'd waited.

She sighed and let her thoughts blow away in the wind. She didn't want to think about what had happened between them in the last few days. Common sense told her that it was like a vacation romance. Too much time and not enough to do.

Like dreams and other insubstantial creations, it could never stand the light of day.

The white sails billowed against the faultless blue sky as the schooner cut through the gray water. They began to pass other vessels as they approached land. Smaller sailboats hailed them and a few larger merchant vessels sent out greetings from their decks.

They were going back to the mainland and their individual lives.

Dana knew that she would be on a plane, flying back to Pittsburgh by the end of the day, and Jeff would be trying to reconcile what had happened with Mattie and Penny's teachers.

Knowing that they were approaching their port, Dana went in search of the girl. Penny was curled up on her bunk with a copy of a music magazine. On the cover was a young man Dana couldn't identify, whose nose was pierced three times.

"Hi," she greeted the girl.

"Hi," Penny returned, putting down the magazine. "You know, Dana, I think that was John Abbott's treasure back there. We might be able to go back and find it and pay off the *Blockade Runner*." She frowned. "But then we'd never see you again."

Dana sat on the bed beside Penny. "That would be great. And if you do it, I promise to come back with the title myself. Okay?"

"But you wouldn't have to come back after that to see Jeff. How would you ever get together?"

It was clearly matchmaking. Dana recalled Jeff's recounting of Penny's efforts.

"Penny," she began, searching for the right words. "I'm going to be married. Your brother will find someone."

"The two of you would be great together." Penny sighed. "And you could sneak me stuff when Jeff wasn't looking."

"Stuff?"

"You know, makeup now, but later it could be car keys and tattoos and . . ."

"I don't think that's going to happen," Dana told her with a rueful smile. "In fact, I know the tattoo part isn't going to happen. Even if your brother and I did—"

"—get together?"

"We're not," Dana assured her.

"Well, I'm going to miss you anyway," Penny told her, hugging her tightly. "I wish you could stay."

Dana didn't reply, but hugged her back tightly. Penny urged her back on deck to watch them enter the river and Dana followed, carefully retaking her seat behind the helm.

She watched as Penny stepped up to the wheel and Jeff let her control the schooner. They talked for a few minutes while he pointed to the mouth of the river they were rapidly approaching.

Dana could see how alike they were, and yet they were so different. Penny and Jeff had shared their loss and had managed to make a new life for themselves. In the process, they seemed to be much closer.

Dana's own childhood had been very different. Growing up in a household with servants and a nanny, she often didn't see her mother and father more than a few minutes each day. Usually in the morning and again in the evening. Sometimes her grandfather looked in on her during the week. Her nannies always assured her that her parents were very busy and not to be bothered unless it was an emergency.

They were not a close family, in the way that Penny and her brother were close. Dana didn't know if her father really loved her mother or if her mother only tolerated her father. She did know that they made a striking couple at charity functions and during promotions for the bank. She knew that her mother played tennis and that her father golfed, but she didn't know what her mother's favorite color was or if her father hated getting up in the morning.

Dana loved her parents, but always from a safe distance. They encouraged her to have her own life and were proud of her decision to marry Branden. She was sure that they loved her.

Her grandfather had always doted on her, but he was larger than life. A big man with massive shoulders and a full head of white hair, she had been alternately terrified and impressed by him. He could do anything. Including intimidate her father and her younger brother, Charlie.

"Almost there," Jeff said as he sat down beside her on the deck.

"Is that the river?" she wondered as they approached the darker water that was crowded with boats and ships of all kinds.

He nodded, pushing the hair back from his eyes when he looked at her. "Penny's going to take it in that far, then we'll switch to the engine so we don't have to try to maneuver in that traffic.''

''She's going to be a good captain herself one day,'' Dana observed.

Jeff nodded. ''She already sees herself piloting freighters to South America.''

''If anyone can, she will.'' Dana considered the girl. ''She's a wonderful person, Jeff. You shouldn't worry that your parents' death has harmed her. She's kind and giving and open, as well as smart. You must be very proud of her.''

''She likes you, too,'' he told her. ''I think it was the makeup. I won't let her wear makeup until she's thirteen, and then only lipstick. That's what Mom had told her.''

''Except for playing at it, I don't blame you. She's just a young girl,'' Dana offered.

''I know,'' he replied, looking back at his sister. ''I know.''

''Why didn't you tell me about my family coming down from Pittsburgh?'' she questioned.

He shrugged. ''I didn't want to spoil the tour of the island for you. I thought if you knew . . .''

''That I would've wanted to leave right away?''

''Yeah.'' He glanced back at her, his gaze narrowed on her face. ''I guess so.''

''Jeff,'' Penny called as they approached the river opening.

"I better go," he said, getting to his feet. "I hope you enjoyed your adventure."

"I won't ever forget it," she promised, looking up at him, wondering if it was a trick of the light that made his eyes turn darker when he looked at her.

"If there isn't another chance for me to say it, Dana, I won't ever forget it either."

Dana couldn't think of anything to say in return so she looked away toward the river traffic. A coward's way out, she knew, but better that than falling on the deck crying.

It was surprising and disconcerting how quickly they followed the river back to their home port. Traffic was heavy, but as evening was falling, the *Blockade Runner* slipped into her berth along the river and Mattie made her fast to her moorings.

There was a small crowd built up on the dock. The falling shadows made it difficult to see who was waiting until they got in closer.

By the time they had docked though, Dana could see that Branden and her grandfather had flown in from Pittsburgh to bring her home. Their worried faces cleared when they saw her, and Branden waved. Her grandfather looked stern but relieved.

The schooner bumped against the dock and the small group surged forward to meet them.

Mattie took Jeff aside privately before the others could reach them. Dana couldn't hear what they were saying, but their expressions were fierce.

"Dana!" Branden called out, pushing his way through the group to reach her side.

She could see her grandfather, standing to the back, waiting for Branden to bring her to him. His face was too shadowed for her to see his features, but she knew he couldn't have been pleased to have to come all the way down there after her.

It made her feel like she did the only time she'd cut school. She'd been caught, and her grandfather's thunderous, disappointed visage was enough to make her break down into tears.

"Dana, I—"

Jeff was at her side, looking down at her. He put one hand on her arm and she turned easily toward him. As though they had known each other a lifetime.

"Come on, Dana." Branden took her arm, drawing her away from the scene. "This joker'll be lucky if we don't press charges against him."

Penny was crying as she silently waved good-bye.

"What you've been through!" Branden continued. "I know you said he was a monster, but Dana, if we'd known, we wouldn't have let you come down here alone."

Over the crowd, Jeff's grim eyes caught hers in the dim overhead light that faced down on them all. It was like a bad play, Dana thought, staring at Jeff and being pulled away by Branden's tug on her arm.

The crowd on the dock had doubled with curious

onlookers until at least fifty people stood between them.

Dana didn't see them. Or hear their buzzing questions. She looked at Jeff. Time stopped. There was only the two of them on the shadowed dock.

"Come along, Dana." Her grandfather broke the spell, wrapping his arm around her as he and Branden hustled her to a waiting car. "You've put us through enough, young lady."

"Nothing happened." Dana found her tongue. "We didn't do anything wrong. It was just a series of accidents."

The old man's eyes stabbed through the twilight to glare at the man whose gaze hadn't left his granddaughter's face. "I don't think you should be defending this man, Dana."

"He didn't kidnap me," Dana told them loudly as the car door closed and they started to leave the dock. "I wanted to go."

"Dana." Her grandfather caught her hands and looked into her troubled face. "You've been through a great strain. You're not yourself. Calm down. Everything's going to be all right. We're going home."

And that was exactly what they did. A chartered plane took them back to Pittsburgh that night rather than waiting until a flight came in the next morning. They distanced themselves from the entire episode as quickly and efficiently as possible.

Dana answered a barrage of questions on the way home. Her hair was a wild mess and her clothes were torn and dirty. She had stuffed her suit into her briefcase and she had no shoes.

What had she done out there all that time? Where had they gone? Had Jeff Satterfield forced her to sail with him from Wilmington? Had he harmed her in any way?

Her grandfather's personal physician met them at her apartment. After a quick physical, which Dana had declared unnecessary, the doctor had pronounced her scruffy but healthy.

Dana had endured as much as she could for one night. She closed her bedroom door in their faces and took a long, hot bath. She tried not to think about everything that had happened as she soaked in the tub. She concentrated on trying to pull herself together and putting the last few days behind her.

Her grandfather was still waiting when she emerged from her room. "You look more like yourself," he commented, his assessing glance sweeping her from head to toe.

She shrugged, feeling leaden. "I'm tired, Grampa. You shouldn't have waited."

"I sent Branden home so that we could talk," he told her briefly. "I called your parents. They were worried, but they couldn't be here tonight."

"The hospital charity auction." Dana smiled and

padded into the kitchen. "Would you like some coffee?"

"Not at this time of night, or rather morning," he refused gruffly. "You won't be able to sleep either if you have some."

"That's probably true," she agreed, "but I won't be able to sleep anyway."

She didn't elaborate. She turned her back to him and started putting coffee into her small espresso machine. Her grandfather took a chair at the table.

"I like what you've done here, Dana," he complimented. "It suits you."

It occurred to Dana that he had never seen her apartment, even though she had lived there five years.

She switched the machine on and looked in her refrigerator. It was bare except for some herbed cheese spread and a few crackers. She dragged them out to the table and sat down with her grandfather.

Chapter Eight

"Are you all right, Dana?" he asked, the lined face concerned despite the doctor's diagnosis.

"I'm fine," she replied calmly, not knowing she could feel so badly and still maintain a good front.

"What you went through . . ."

"It really was just a series of accidents, Grampa," she reiterated. "I wanted to go out on the schooner to get a feeling of what it was like to go on a cruise. The engine failed. I fell overboard and there was a storm. We came back to port."

"Dana, correct me if I'm wrong," her grandfather began, "but haven't you and your brother always had weak stomachs? You've never been able to abide the water."

"They came out with a patch that you wear behind

144

your ear,'' she explained. ''I knew I was going to have to be around boats, so I wore one down there.''

''You're a clever girl, Dana. That was what happened last time, wasn't it? But you outsmarted the man this time. Good for you!''

He sat back, studying her face, not saying anything else until she came back with her espresso.

She studied the wildflower pattern on her small cup and traced the edge with what was left of her fingernail. Idly, she considered that she needed a manicure.

''That man . . .''

''Jeff Satterfield,'' she added, neatly spreading cheese on a cracker, knowing she couldn't force it into her mouth if her life depended on it.

It was all image, though. The image that she was cool and untouched by her ordeal. That nothing that had happened had made any difference to her. Life would go on as it always had before she had spent time on the *Blockade Runner*.

''Jeff Satterfield.'' He nodded. ''Is that the same man with the loan from our bank?''

''Yes. I plan to extend his loan for the needed repairs on the schooner and to cover office expenses.''

He stared at her. ''Are you besotted with the man?''

Besotted? She smiled at her grandfather, for once

seeing him as an older man with some very old-fashioned ideas.

"I'm not sure if that would cover it, but . . ."

"You can't be serious, Dana. I won't let you mix a bad personal decision with a bad business decision."

Dana stared back at him. "Does that mean you won't back me because I was gone a few days? Or because you think he's a bad risk?"

"What about Branden?" Her grandfather tacked as hard as Jeff had during the storm front. "What about your lives together? Are you going to throw away everything for a miscreant like that?"

"I'm not going to throw away anything," she assured him brightly. "I respect Jeff Satterfield and I think his cruises will do well. I have from the beginning."

"I know." He sighed heavily.

"And he's not a miscreant," she defended. "He's a very hardworking businessman who's had a few unfortunate turns. I still think he can make it."

"So there's nothing between you but business?" Her grandfather's sharp eyes watched her carefully.

Dana sipped her espresso. "It was an adventure, Grampa. Nothing more. I'm home now. Nothing's changed."

Her grandfather stood as though he was feeling the weight of his seventy years. "I won't let you do this, Dana. This man was a moderate risk before. I feel

he's become a bad risk. A few 'unfortunate accidents' seem to be a way of life for him.''

He looked down at her with loving eyes. ''If
there's nothing between you but business, Dana, then
let's put an end to it right now. Before it becomes
something more.''

Dana looked at him with tears in her eyes. Her
grandfather had never denied her a choice in the
business. He had always kept himself strictly neutral
in her affairs.

''What are you saying?'' she demanded as a tight
coil of fear and love squeezed her throat.

''If you put this before the committee, I will vote
to deny it,'' he explained baldly. ''I love you, Dana.
Get some rest. You'll see I'm right about this one.''

He kissed her forehead lightly, then turned and
walked out of her door.

Dana sat where she was, numb. She imagined him
climbing into the limousine and being driven home.

He had as good as told her that Jeff's loan would
be refused. If he actively fought her on the project,
it would be the death of Jeff's business.

Nothing had changed, she told herself frantically,
looking in her bedroom mirror as tears rolled down
her cheeks. Why couldn't everyone see that?

Yet as she sat at her desk two weeks later, she
realized that everything had changed. Nothing was
the same.

She had technically gone through the usual paces

of her life. She'd seen Branden and driven out for dinner with her parents.

There had been a weekend house party for the bank's senior officers. She'd talked and laughed and worn a new dress that everyone complimented.

She'd gone about her job as though she'd never been gone. Loans were approved and disapproved. She'd flown to Chicago to meet with a group of investors who wanted to remodel one of the city's great old hotels.

But all of the food was ashes in her mouth and all of the music was the sound of the water and the birds. Every time the phone rang at her desk, she expected to hear Jeff's voice. Every night became an eternity.

Yet, it was like she was watching someone else do those things. Someone else was living her life while she stood off on the sidelines and wondered what had happened.

When had it changed? Why had she become the pale wraith of herself that flitted through the dark corners of her mind?

She finally made room in her schedule to visit her rented warehouse space, but even working with her furniture couldn't make her feel as though she were still alive. It was as though a part of her had died when she'd walked off the *Blockade Runner* that evening.

It didn't take long to understand that she had lied

to her grandfather. She *was* besotted with Jeff Satterfield. Every day when her alarm clock went off, her first thought was of him.

She had picked up the phone a dozen times to call the *Blockade Runner* office and ask whoever was there if everything was all right. Just on the off chance that it might be Jeff who picked up the phone.

Maybe it was the sea air. Or the blue skies. Or his arms around her. Or the feel of his lips on hers.

She didn't know what it was, but it had robbed a part of her that she knew she could never have back again. Dana Eller wasn't the same person, after the cruise, that she had been before the storm and Stump Island.

It hit her hard and cold one night as she was lying in her bed trying to sleep.

She was in love with Jeff Satterfield. She wanted him to hold her and teach her to steer his boat. She wanted him to laugh with her and tell her to look for her dreams. She wanted him to flash those cold gray eyes at her when he was angry and wanted to see the wind toss his dark hair as he stood on the deck of the schooner.

Did that mean she didn't love Branden? she wondered, looking at her fiancé as he escorted her to the opera late one Thursday evening.

They were about the same height, Branden with brown hair and brown eyes. He kept in shape by playing handball and tennis a few times a week and he looked good in his evening clothes. He had been satisfied with her explanation of what had happened between her and Jeff, and they had gone on as though nothing had happened.

And the old Dana would have been satisfied with that as well. But the Dana who'd changed wondered why the passion between them seemed forced. They went to the right places and did the right things. They looked good together, as her parents did, but suddenly it wasn't enough.

Branden caught her staring at him in the cab on the way home from the theater.

"What's wrong?" he asked, touching the bright diamond on her finger.

"I don't know," she whispered truthfully.

"I think I do," he provided, slipping his arm around her shoulders and drawing her close to him.

She knew it was wrong to compare the two men. She didn't really mean to but it happened nonetheless.

Where Jeff's kiss had made her worry and wonder for a year before she saw him again, Branden's left her unmoved. He was tender. He was gentle. But he wasn't the right man.

She opened her eyes and they looked at each other for a long moment before he withdrew.

"It's him, isn't it?" he asked, a cheerful front to his voice. He looked away from her to the darkened interior of the cab.

''Yes.'' She couldn't lie anymore. ''I'm afraid so.''

''So.'' He sighed. ''What now?''

''I don't know.''

''Does he know how you feel?'' he wondered. ''Does he care for you, Dana?''

''I'm not sure,'' she admitted slowly.

''But you are sure about your feelings?''

''Yes.'' She looked at him, pushing a tear from the corner of her eye with a careless, gloved finger.

''Well.'' He sighed again and kissed her cheek. ''If you change your mind . . . We make a good team, Dana.''

''I know,'' she confessed sorrowfully.

''Are you going back down there?'' he asked.

''I don't know,'' she answered truthfully, not having thought that far ahead. ''I don't know what's going to happen yet.''

She didn't tell her parents or her grandfather. She couldn't find the words and she didn't want her new and raw emotions subjected to their scrutiny yet.

Did she have a future with Jeff Satterfield? What kind of life could they have together? Did he care about her? How serious was her commitment to him?

She asked herself those questions a thousand times a day. She didn't need anyone else to grill her on the subject.

She came into the bank after having lunch with an old school friend and found a note on her desk. The decision had come down from the committee. She had called her grandfather's bluff on the *Blockade Runner*'s loan. But the committee had declined to invest anything else in what they loosely termed "a bad association."

Even worse for Jeff, they were calling in the loan on the schooner. He would have thirty days to pay back everything, or the bank would claim its property.

Her first thought was to pick up the phone and tell Jeff what was coming his way. He had a right to know, and with a few more days . . .

That wasn't the answer. She put down the receiver, wanting to have the excuse to hear Jeff's voice, but pausing to think before she did something she would regret.

He would never be able to raise that kind of cash. A few days, a few weeks. She had seen his statements and she knew he was barely making ends meet.

For a long time after she'd hung up the phone, she sat and stared into space, thinking about the problem and trying to decide what to do.

An answer came to her at once and she rejected it offhand, knowing Jeff would never accept it. But the more she considered it, the more she knew that it was the right answer.

She would go back down to Wilmington and break the news to Jeff. Then, she would offer him the help of a qualified investor: herself. With her savings and the trust from her grandmother, she would be able to keep the *Blockade Runner* afloat.

She believed in his business. She believed in him. It could work.

But first, she would have to face the lion in his den. Her grandfather wouldn't be fooled when he knew that she was going back.

"Is he in?" Dana asked his secretary after making the trek up to the top office.

"He's in," Grace told her. "Maybe you can put him in a better mood. He's biting your father's head off right now."

"Maybe I should wait," Dana quailed.

"I don't think so," Grace responded, opening the door.

"Thanks."

"Your dad can use your help," Grace whispered.

The chairman's office had always had a somber, serious air. When Dana was small, she'd spent time there with her grandfather on her days out of school.

She would sit in his chair that looked out of the big window at the sprawling city below and pretend that she was locked in a high tower and that a handsome prince was coming to save her.

Overwhelmed by the size of everything and the power of the man who'd sat behind the desk, she'd spent those days quietly doing as she was told.

When she walked into the office as an adult, she

felt the same urge to run and hide. She had come as close as she'd ever come to talking back to James Eller the morning she'd come back from Wilmington. But pretending and hiding wasn't the answer anymore.

Father and son had been quarreling but they stopped when they looked up and saw Dana walking across the dark carpet toward them.

"Hello, Dana," her father said with a bitter twist to his mouth. "I haven't seen much of you lately."

"I know, Dad," she said quietly. "We'll have to do lunch."

"Dana," her grandfather acknowledged her beneath the white thundercloud of his impressive eyebrows. "You're looking better."

"I'm fine, Grampa."

"What brings you up here, young lady? I've had the feeling the last few weeks that you've been avoiding me."

Her father mumbled something and turned away from them toward the window.

James Eller glanced at his only son, but didn't comment on whatever he'd said. Dana looked between them and wondered what they were quarreling about this time.

"I haven't been avoiding you," Dana replied easily. "But I am thinking about taking a week of my vacation time."

"Oh?"

"I think I could use a break," Dana told him.

"This wouldn't have anything to do with that Satterfield man, would it?" he wondered briefly.

Dana glanced at her father then looked back at her grandfather. "I'm going down to tell him about the loan. It might give him time to find another way."

"I don't think you should get mixed up in this, Dana," he persisted. "You did what you could for the man. Leave it alone."

"I'm already mixed up in it, Grampa. I can't let this happen without offering to help."

"Offering to help?" James Eller raised a cool eyebrow as he glared at her. "What exactly does that mean?"

Dana hadn't meant to say that much but it was already out. "I'm going to offer to become his partner. I think the operation is viable. I have other investments. *Blockade Runner* would just be another."

"I wouldn't have thought you could be such a sentimental fool."

Her grandfather sat down at his desk and started to sift through piles of paperwork on his neatly organized desk. "This isn't a good time for you to take a week, Dana. Maybe in another month or so."

"Grampa," Dana began, ready to do battle.

"Oh, for Pete's sake, Father! Let her go! You can't control everyone's life."

Dana and her grandfather turned to look at Charles

Eller. Dana had never heard her father talk to her grandfather in that tone.

"I don't think this involves you," James told his son coldly.

"You're wrong, Father. I am president of this bank. I oversee employees and the daily running of the bank. Dana has my permission to take her week off and go help her friend. She doesn't need your permission."

"I think you're overstepping your bounds," the chairman roared. "I can fire you today. Then you won't be overseeing anything but the unemployment line."

"Is that what you're prepared to do? If so, I'll expect that letter on my desk by the close of the business day. But while I am the president," he began, turning to his daughter, "take your week, Dana. Go when you need to. Live your life."

Dana glanced between father and son and noticed for the first time that her grandfather was beginning to look tired and perhaps not quite so tall and overpowering.

"Go on," her grandfather said with a shrug. "Ruin your life if you have to."

Dana hurried out of the office, not wanting to hear whatever else would be said between them. She had known that there had always been a certain bitterness between the two men, but she had never heard her father express himself in that manner. To defy her grandfather after all those years! And on her account!

It showed her again that her thoughts on the boat were true. She didn't know her parents well enough to know what to expect from them. Maybe she could remedy that situation, if they'd let her.

"Well?" Grace breathed softly as the big door closed behind Dana.

"It might be the start of a new era," Dana told her. "If they don't kill each other."

Grace looked glumly back at her computer as she waited to hear what came next.

Dana had her assistant call for plane reservations. She picked up her purse and headed for home.

She would be leaving the next evening, Thursday, and in the meantime, she decided that she would spend her time on one of her projects. Dressed in her oldest jeans and a faded shirt, she walked to her storage building and pushed herself into her work.

Dana arrived at the airport in Wilmington late Thursday night. There was only one person at the counter. The rest of the airport was shut down tight. She'd arrived with a fairly large group of people who'd dissipated quickly when friends and family had found them.

She hadn't called ahead to tell Jeff that she was coming. She wasn't sure what her welcome would be, not sure if Jeff would appreciate the idea of her interfering.

She smiled when she saw the taxi parked by the front door. The driver was asleep at the wheel, his hat tipped forward on his head. Obviously, he hadn't had his fare for the day.

He was startled when she knocked on the window, but his face lit up when he recognized her.

"Hey! What brings you back down this way?"

"I had to come back on business, Earl," she explained. "How about a ride?"

He nodded. "Goin' out to the *Blockade Runner* office?"

"Not this time," she replied quietly, looking away from him as she spoke. "I'm going to the Ramada on Fifth Street. Know it?"

"Sure do," he answered enthusiastically. "Hop on in here. Won't take but a minute."

Dana knew better than that. The man drove like a snail, but it was good to see a familiar face. She climbed in the back of the taxi while he stowed her travel bag, then listened to him rattle off what sights they passed and everything that had happened while she had been gone.

Had it been a month? she wondered, looking out at the lights on the river, wondering where in that darkness Jeff was that night.

"How long will you be stayin' this time?" Earl wondered when they reached the hotel.

"Probably not more than a day or so," she replied,

not certain herself. Wanting to think that she might be staying longer.

"Give me a call if you need to go somewheres," he told her with a pull on his cap. "You could be my one fare tomorrow, too."

She laughed and gave him a generous tip with his fare. "Thanks. I'll do that."

Dana signed in at the front desk. The lobby was quiet. There was only one other couple just coming in as she was picking up her key.

Her room was on the top floor. She rode the elevator up, clutching her overnight bag, wondering what Jeff would say when he saw her. Would he be pleased? Would he be annoyed that she had come back to help?

Did he feel anything at all for her? That was the question that plagued her. Of course, she could salvage her pride. She only needed to tell him that she'd heard about the loan and decided to come back down to make sure things went okay.

She could offer him her qualified investor without him ever knowing that it was her.

She didn't need to tell him about the terrible loneliness she'd discovered couldn't be consumed by her work once she'd left him. He didn't need to know the long nights she'd stared up at the ceiling, wondering if he was thinking about her.

It took courage to follow a dream. To risk everything. She still wasn't sure she had that kind of courage. She had toyed with the idea of giving up her job and working on her furniture full time but she had balked at that kind of risk.

Would she be able to risk even more to tell Jeff how she felt? To dare to consider that they might make their lives a partnership in every sense of the word?

It had taken everything she had to stand up to her grandfather about making the trip down there to help him. Now that she was there, it was so much more complicated and difficult to imagine seeing him again.

What would she say? How would he react?

She was tired when she swiped the card through the security lock on her room door. It opened easily and she slipped inside, dropping her bag on the floor and shutting the door behind her.

Her room overlooked the river and the drapes had been left open to view the lights up and down the long waterway. Like diamonds they sparkled, glinting back off the smooth black sheen that was the water. She left the lights off and walked to the cool glass to watch for a moment.

The lights made her move her hand over the place that had worn Branden's diamond for so long. There was an indentation and a white mark where the ring had been until two weeks before when she'd given it back.

Branden had taken it well. It made her wonder if

he'd questioned their relationship as well. Even though he'd made her promise that if things didn't work out between her and Jeff that she would come back to him.

She knew she wouldn't do that. Falling in love with Jeff had made her realize that there was so much more than just doing well together. There was laughter and that sweet fire of his kisses.

Dana sighed and turned on the lights, closing the drapes and undressing. She headed for the shower, the stinging hot water reviving her enough that she recalled she hadn't eaten since early that morning.

An attack of nerves had almost made her cancel the flight at the last minute. She couldn't eat, hadn't slept the night before, and her brain was running through a thousand scenarios at once.

Jeff saw her in the street and shouted for her to leave.

Jeff saw her and acted like he'd never seen her before.

She closed her eyes as the water flowed over her face and neck.

Jeff saw her and swept her into his arms. He kissed her and she knew that everything was going to be all right.

Jeff told her that he wanted to spend the rest of his life with her, that he was willing to risk everything if she would stay with him.

The last two were her personal favorites.

He might not care for her as she believed that she cared for him. She sighed. But what if he did?

After her shower, she slipped on an emerald satin robe that her brother had given her for Christmas, wishing that she could have talked to Charlie. They weren't especially close, but he had a devil-may-care attitude that she needed to emulate just then.

He spent most of his time managing the bank's overseas holdings simply to avoid her grandfather and his dictates.

Charlie would have told her to show up at the docks the next day with her cutest outfit and a winning attitude and knock them dead, especially Jeff Satterfield.

Charlie was handsome and ingratiating. If she had his easy line of patter, she wouldn't be standing around in a hotel room wondering what Jeff would say when she saw him.

She dried her hair and brushed it slowly, sitting in front of the big window again in the dark. Even late at night, ships were moving in and out of the harbor. She could see their slow progress skimming down the water, their lights making them look like Christmas decorations in motion.

Wondering if it was too late for room service, she picked up the phone and there was a knock at the door. She looked down at her robe and bare feet, but she was presentable. She tightened the sash at her waist and stepped to the door, leaving the lights off behind her.

''Yes?'' she asked, holding the door only slightly ajar.

''Danny!''

Chapter Nine

The fierce whisper of her name started her heart pounding like a wild thing, but before she could move or speak, he had wrapped his arms around her, almost dragging her off her feet against his chest.

His mouth was on hers and a bright blinding need enveloped her. She let go of the door and held him tightly.

"Jeff," she breathed when his kisses would let her. She heard the door slam shut as he moved them into the hotel room.

"I've missed you," he murmured, his fingers tangling in her still damp hair. "You've been gone forever."

"Jeff." She tried to say his name but it came out more like an excited croak. "Jeff," she repeated

164

more steadily, her hands reaching his shoulders, holding him back for a moment so that she could see his face.

He looked stricken in the dim light. "Danny, I'm sorry," he apologized at once, his hands dropping to his sides. His eyes stayed on her face. "I promised myself when Earl called and told me that you were here that I wouldn't do this. I just wanted to talk to you, to see you again. But when I saw your face . . ."

She didn't know what to say. Her heart was so full of so many things and her brain was whirling with the sound and feel of him.

He took her hands in his, glancing down at her fingers after a moment. "Your ring," he wondered, pulling her after him to stand in the light from the window. "Danny, where's your engagement ring?"

"I gave it back," she replied in a shaky voice. "Branden and I aren't going to be married."

"Why, Danny?" he questioned in a less-than-steady voice.

"Jeff," she whispered huskily, turning from him to face the window and the river below. "Have you ever seen anything more beautiful?"

His arms came slowly around her, his chest warm at her back. "Nothing," he answered, feathering light kisses down the side of her neck.

She sighed and relaxed in his arms. "I've never seen so many lights," she spoke, her voice a little less certain as her brain reeled and she trembled at his touch.

"Me either," he acknowledged, his hands beginning to move slowly through her hair.

Dana saw their faint reflection in the darkened window. His mouth brushed her ear, tracing the delicate outline. She could hear the sound of his heart beating with her own.

"And there's a big purple moon out there," she said, knowing he wasn't listening.

"Yeah," he agreed, intent on turning her slightly, his lips working their magic to reach her mouth.

She smiled and he kissed the curve of her lips.

"Hey," he muttered, sitting down suddenly in the big chair near the window and taking her with him. "Don't think I don't know what you just said."

"I thought you came to talk to me," she reminded him, threading her fingers through his thick hair, feeling the muscles react in his neck and shoulders.

"I did," he replied softly, looking into her eyes that sparkled like gemstones in the dim light. "How are you, Danny? How was your flight? But first, kiss me, Danny, please."

She complied, forgetting everything for several moments while her blood boiled and her senses were shattered by his gentle caresses and sweet, intoxicating words.

"I know now why women waited years for their

sailors to come back home,'' she said when she could.

''It wasn't for the conversation,'' he promised her with a knowing look.

She laughed and kissed him quickly. ''Jeff, I—''

He paused in his tender ministrations and dared a look at her. ''You . . . ? Yes?''

She closed her eyes and shook her head. ''I came back down because of the bank. They've decided against your loan and they're going to give you thirty days to pay off the first loan. I want to help.''

''You have,'' he told her, wrapping her closely against him. ''Immeasurably. Beyond words.''

''I mean I want to help you find a way to stay in business. A partner,'' she explained, losing her train of thought while he kissed her, then regaining it. ''You need a partner.''

''Do you have anyone in mind?'' he whispered hopefully.

''Well, yes.'' She pushed back from him. ''I was thinking that I could become your partner.''

''Danny!'' He kissed her soundly. ''That sounds like the greatest proposal in the world to me!''

''I have some money saved, and my grandmother left a trust in my name.''

''Wait a minute!'' He stopped suddenly and stared at her. ''Are you talking about giving me your money? A business partnership?''

She blinked her eyes, hating that he had withdrawn from her. "Of course. I, uh—"

"Danny, I want *you*." His hands framed her face. "I want you more than any business. I want you in my arms. Do you want me like that?"

Dana thought back to her original proposal, wondering if she had said something wrong.

"Of course I want you! And I can help you save your boat and your business. Is that what you mean?"

He picked her up again, his arms warm and strong around her, then set her down on the bed.

"Danny, I don't want your money."

He was standing in front of her, tall and real, but she couldn't see his face or his eyes in the darkness.

"I just wanted to help you. So you wouldn't lose your dream," she volunteered.

His touch traced the soft curve of her face. "Coming back here is enough for me. You don't need to put money into the business."

Dana was confused. "I want to help. The money is just sitting there in the bank. We can draw up papers if it makes you feel better. You can pay me back like a loan company."

Jeff knelt quickly on the floor beside her and took her hands in his. "Danny, did you come back for me? Or for the investment?"

She desperately wanted to say the right thing. She

wished she could know what he was thinking. What did he want her to say?

"When they told me about the loan, I tried to think of some way to salvage your business," she skirted the immediate question in his voice. "I came up with the idea of a qualified investor and I came down to tell you."

"So, it was a business proposal and not a marriage proposal?"

Dana gasped. "I—I didn't think, I mean, in your position . . ."

"You didn't think I would want to take one without the other?" he murmured.

Something was wrong. Cold reality began to seep into Dana's heart. What was he saying?

"I don't think we're talking on the same wavelength, Jeff," she told him in a shaky voice.

He kissed the tips of her fingers, then stood up, taking her with him.

"I think we both know what I'm talking about, Danny. You want me to be someone you can show off to your family as being successful, whatever it takes. That way, they can't object too strongly."

"No, I—"

"I won't take your money, sweetheart. I appreciate that you came all the way back down here, but I can work it out."

"Jeff, I . . ." She faltered as she touched his arm.

"I have to take a cruise out tonight," he told her,

his voice sounding hushed and empty of emotion. "I just stopped by for a few minutes to see you."

"I do care about you, Jeff," she blurted out frantically. "I wanted to help you."

"I understand, Danny," he replied carefully, slowly caressing her face. "I'll be back. Will you be here?"

"I—I don't know," she responded, confused and uncertain about what had just happened between them. She needed time to think.

"Okay." He kissed her lightly and touched the silver locket around her throat. Then he moved away from her. "I'll see you later then, Danny."

The door closed quietly and Dana sank down on the bed, desperately going over every word, every touch between them.

What had gone wrong? What had she said? It wasn't supposed to be happening that way. They were supposed to end up together.

She had wanted to help him, but in her single-minded determination, she had forgotten to tell him that she loved him.

Or had she?

Hadn't she been waiting to hear the words from him first, just in case she was wrong about his feelings? Hadn't she talked around what he was saying because she was still afraid to give up everything for that dream, dreading the consequences of disaster?

Dana dressed quickly, throwing on the clothes she

had just changed, and ran from the hotel room. She knew she couldn't wait for Earl. There wasn't time.

After receiving directions from the front desk clerk, she ran down the street that fronted the river, toward the docks. The night was warm and damp and filled with noises from the traffic on the water.

As though there had been a homing beacon, she ran directly to the slip where the *Runner* should have been docked, but it was gone.

Mattie was there, just getting into his pickup truck, when he saw her run up to the dark, empty place on the dock.

"Dana Eller?" he queried, surprised, narrowing his gaze through the pale light.

"Mattie!" she managed, breathlessly. She bent over, trying to catch her breath to say something more.

"What are you doing down here?" he wondered, scratching his head. "Does Jeff know you're here?"

"Yes." She gasped, a sharp pain in her side. "Where is he?"

"He's probably gone by now," he told her with a quick glance at his watch. "He had to moor the *Runner* down at the other end of the river while they do repairs on this slip. But he was going out on a tour half an hour ago."

"Let's go!" she demanded, getting into the truck and slamming the door. "Maybe we can still catch him."

Mattie followed her as fast as he could, but the truck took a few tries to start up. He revved the old engine, daring a quick look at her from the corner of his eye.

"Even if he's gone," she speculated once they were moving, "we can call him on the radio, right?"

He shifted gears. "Well, that might be a problem. The radio went out yesterday and there wasn't time—"

"You mean we can't call him?"

"He's only going to be gone for a few days."

"Step on it, Mattie," she advised tartly. "We don't *have* a few days."

"What's the matter, Dana? Is it something I can help you with until Jeff gets back?"

"I have to tell him that I love him, Mattie," she said softly, but with a trace of iron in her tone. "I forgot that part. But there's still time."

"Yes, ma'am!" he yelled, giving a small whoop afterward. He put his foot down hard on the gas pedal and the truck gave a lurch forward.

All the slips along the river looked the same to Dana, but Mattie followed the route with knowing eyes, finally stopping between two other large sailing vessels.

"Too late," he uttered angrily. "He's gone. Sorry, Dana."

For a moment, she couldn't speak, couldn't think. All those things she should have said welled up in her and wanted to free themselves, screaming, from her brain.

"It's all right, Mattie," she said carefully, not wanting to release those wraiths that howled within her. "He'll be back."

"Sure he will," the older man assured her gently. "He'll be back in a few days and things can be just fine between you. Life is good sometimes, ain't it?"

"Mattie." She looked at him with her heart in her eyes. "Did he tell you that he loves me? Did he say anything about me?"

"We-ll, no. Not exactly," he answered slowly, trying to say what she wanted to hear but not wanting to lie to her either.

"Oh."

"But Jeff's not one to wear his heart on his sleeve. Know what I mean? He keeps himself to himself most of the time. But I know him, Dana. He cares about you. He cares about you a lot."

Dana looked at the empty space of the mooring slip and felt the weight of her elation crushing down on her. There were thousands of lights out on the dark currents of the river. Any of them could be the *Blockade Runner.*

"Could you take me back to my hotel?" she wondered in a small voice.

Mattie started the truck slowly, wanting to reassure her. He rambled on about Jeff and his feelings and how he could tell that the man was in love with her, but when they had reached the hotel, Dana got out of the truck and looked at him sadly.

''Good-bye, Mattie. Thanks.''

He worried his lower lip with his teeth. ''Dana, don't let somethin' an old fool like me tells you drive you away. Jeff needs you, darlin'. It'll all work out. You'll see.''

She smiled and he wanted to cry, watching her walk into the hotel.

He made up his mind to see her again in the morning. Maybe they could borrow a boat and catch up with Jeff. Maybe he could just get her to stay until Jeff came back to port.

But before he got to the hotel in the morning, she was gone.

Dana knew she couldn't go on pretending that nothing had happened to her. She made her plans on the plane as she headed back for Pittsburgh again.

Her first stop was the bank, where she tendered her resignation. It took only three minutes on her word processor to end her career.

She didn't bother taking it to her father personally. Instead she gave it to his assistant and she cleared out her desk, promising to send for the rest of her things in a few days.

Her grandfather, in a rare moment of regret, had his driver take him to her apartment, only to find that she had left and given no forwarding address. He picked up the car phone and called her mother, but no one else had heard from Dana either.

Two weeks later, by the time Charlie Eller flew in from Paris, the family was frantic with worry. There was no word from the police. No one of Dana's description had been admitted to any of the hospitals. A private detective had been combing the city for her but there were no clues.

It took Charlie only an hour to find his sister. He opened the door of the low-rent shop in the artsy district of the city and a small bell tinkled, announcing him.

''I'm not quite ready to open yet,'' Dana said, then paused, looking up at him. ''Charlie!''

He grinned and hugged his sister close, ignoring the stained jeans and shirt full of sawdust. ''Hi, there. Anything unusual happen that you'd like to tell me about?''

''Well, not really,'' she hedged. ''How'd you know where to find me?''

''I've known your secret fetish for working with furniture for years,'' he admitted, walking around the shop and admiring the beginning of her handiwork.

''How?'' she asked, confused.

He laughed. ''I have a friend who runs a gallery two doors up from here, next to the coffeehouse. He saw you down here and asked me if you were slumming or if you'd gone insane.''

Dana cleaned her hands on a rag self-consciously. "What are you doing home?"

"Your big birthday bash is tomorrow, remember?"

"Oh, no!" she replied, stricken. "I forgot."

"You forgot your birthday," he muttered with a shake of his head. "Good. I wanted to keep your very expensive present that I brought you back from England anyway."

"I—I don't know what to do, Charlie," she admitted.

"You could start by letting everyone know that you're okay," he supplied. "The family is worried to death about you, Dana. They have the National Guard and the Secret Service out looking for you."

"I didn't think—"

"That much is obvious."

"You didn't tell them that you knew where I was?" she ventured, ashamed that she had caused them such grief.

"No." He stared at her. "I thought you should do that. You're the one who ran away."

"I didn't run away," she argued.

"Oh, no?" He picked up a small stool, then sat down on it, looking up at her. "What would you call all this then, Dana?"

She looked around herself and knew there had to be some way to explain. She simply didn't know where to start.

"You don't have six months to live or something, do you?" he wondered, frowning.

"Maybe," she answered with a short laugh that ended with a hiccup of tears. "Oh, Charlie!"

He stood up and put his arm around her. They walked down to the coffeehouse where he wheedled all of it out of her. She cried and drank three cups of espresso, using his handkerchief and two napkins.

"All right," he summed it all up when she'd finished and blown her nose for the last time. "So, you fell in love with this schooner captain who told you that you should be willing to go for what you want out of life, but then you got cold feet on the important part. Him. Instead, you came back here and messed up the rest of your life. Does that about cover it?"

She nodded and sniffled. "It's hopeless."

"Nothing that can't be set right with a wave of my magic wand." He smiled at her. "First off, come home with me. Right now. Let everyone know what you're doing and that you're all right. I'll stand there with you and hold your hand if you want me to."

"I can do that," she said. "I was just afraid that they'd talk me out of it."

"If they ever saw this place..." He glanced around him at the dimly lit café. "I think they'd probably try. But Dana, they love you. They might give you some static, but eventually, they'll support your decision. They'd support whatever you wanted to do.''

''I know.'' She started crying again and blew her nose.

''About the schooner captain.'' He sighed. ''Love doesn't always work out. But every great artist has had a romantic catalyst that changed their lives. Maybe he was yours.''

Dana walked back to the shop with him and they talked about Paris and his trip to Tibet. She thought about how much she would have liked for Jeff to meet her brother. They could have been friends.

She took a shower and changed clothes while Charlie phoned home to let everyone know that he had found her and was bringing her back for her birthday.

She didn't feel festive enough for the bright green dress she'd laid out to wear, but it *was* a party. And she had a lot of apologies to make to her family.

Dreading going back, she shored up her courage, putting her hair up on her head with two silver barrettes and using makeup with a slightly heavier hand. She put on her dress, like a suit of armor, smiling when it swished against her legs instead of clanking.

Maybe Charlie was right, she thought, looking at her slightly thinner face in the mirror on her makeup table. Maybe her love for Jeff was just a catalyst and not something that was meant to be in the real world.

Maybe it was something she would have to let go. Maybe she would have to forget about him.

She sighed. Maybe she would have to have part of her brain and all of her heart removed to accomplish those impossible tasks.

Working with her furniture night and day for the past two weeks, setting up her shop—none of it was as satisfying as she had thought it would be to her. At the end of the day or early in the morning, it was still just her and her heart, and they were both crying out for Jeff.

''I'm ready,'' she greeted her brother as she descended the old wooden stairs from her living space above the shop.

''You look great,'' he admired, taking her arm. ''Has it occurred to you that you could use your connections, the people we both know, to sell your furniture to a higher-class crowd? In other words, the ones with the money?''

Dana locked the shop door and followed him to his car, listening to his plan for networking her dream. She smiled and nodded but knew she couldn't do it. Everything was too new, too frightening to push out into the street. It would be like putting a newborn child out in a spotlight and telling it to perform.

But he talked and she listened and remarked at the appropriate times. Her thoughts were far away on the coast with a schooner and the captain who piloted her. They were probably heading out for the Atlantic, somewhere looking for treasure or exploring the ghost town on Stump Island.

When Charlie pulled into the long driveway, she began to panic. The heavy wrought-iron gate closed behind them and she knew she had no choice but to stand up to her worst fears.

What was she going to say? How could she possibly explain?

The house was ablaze with lights. They illuminated the new roses and the fine pink marble that fronted the wide double doors. The diamond drops of the chandelier in the huge front foyer showed through the tall window above the door.

"Take a deep breath." Charlie steadied her with words and a strong handclasp. "Smile and knock 'em dead."

The doors opened as the car slowed down and stopped. Her mother, in a black evening dress, looking worried and suspiciously tearful, walked out, holding her father's hand.

Her grandfather, in his twenty-year-old tuxedo, followed them, looking angry and gruff like a dark thundercloud.

There was someone else standing behind them. A man in a tuxedo whose dark hair was combed back from a lean face. Whose gray eyes burned holes in her soul.

Jeff.

"You didn't tell me," she hissed at her brother as she tightened her hold on his hand.

"You didn't ask," he replied, perfectly at ease. "Shall we go?"

Marcia Eller stepped forward, her expressive green eyes sweeping her daughter's face. She hugged Dana tightly to her.

"I love you, Dana. Whatever's happened," she began, drawing her husband to her side, "we just want you to come home."

Charles Eller hugged his wife and daughter together until both women were crying. His father cleared his throat and the three moved apart.

"Enough of this wailing! Dana." James Eller touched his granddaughter's arm with a careful hand. "Can you forgive an old man his stubbornness?"

"Grampa," she cried, and hugged him tightly. "I love you."

"What about me?" Charlie stepped up from the curb. "Don't I get tears and forgiveness?"

"Bah!" James Eller mockingly cuffed his grandson on the side of his head. "I should switch you for knowing where she was and not telling anyone! Is that any way to run an organization?"

"Oh, how rude!" Marcia Eller stepped away from the door. "There's someone here to see you, Dana. He's come a long way."

"And nearly took my head off," her grandfather added.

"So, we'll just go into the library and the two of you can . . ." Marcia paused for aid from the rest of her family when it was obvious her daughter and her friend hadn't heard a word she'd said.

"Let's just go in, Mother." Charlie herded them all away from the door, shutting it behind them.

"Jeff," Dana said, still standing on the sidewalk in front of her home. "I can't believe you're here."

He looked heartbreakingly handsome, with his smoky eyes and dark hair. The lines of his face were taut and he didn't say a word.

"I'm sorry I had to leave before you got back," she apologized, beginning to wonder why he was there. "Was it a good trip?"

"Did you tell Mattie that you loved me?" he demanded in an uncompromising voice.

"What?"

"Did you come down to the docks to look for me and tell Mattie that you loved me?" he repeated.

"Well, I . . ." she stammered, looking for a way out and finding nothing but the reality of him standing in front of her.

He was close enough to touch. Her eyes searched his, hoping for some clue to his own feelings. But they were depthless, like the sea.

"Yes," she finally pronounced in a voice that wavered at first, then added in a stronger tone, "Yes. I did tell Mattie that I loved you."

"Danny," he whispered, gathering her in his arms and kissing her.

"Jeff, I—"

"I love you, Danny. Don't ever leave me again. Nothing means anything without you."

For an instant, Dana couldn't believe her ears, then suddenly she realized that it had to be true. She wrapped her arms tightly around his neck and lost herself in the rich promise of his kisses.

He took her hand finally, not daring to let her go when he'd been lucky enough to find her, and led her to a small stone bench near the rosebushes.

"It's been hard on your family this past week," he told her, sitting beside her on the bench.

"I know," she whispered with a sparkle of tears in her eyes. "I was wrong. But when I found that little shop and started working . . ."

"You started making your furniture?" He hugged her tightly and kissed her again. "That's great! Can we transport it to Wilmington? We have a huge market for handmade stuff. I think . . . what's wrong?"

"You're going to have to go back to work as a cruise captain, aren't you? You've lost the *Blockade Runner*."

He kissed her hand as though it were made of fragile china. "I'm so sorry, Danny. It was my pride that was talking that night. I convinced myself that you only wanted me if I was successful like your family."

"I love you," she said again, loving the feel of the words on her lips. "I'm sorry I couldn't say it that night until you were gone. I don't care what you do or how much money you have."

"But you'd miss me if I was gone all the time?" he prompted.

"I'd die a slow and meaningless death every time you left. But I'd wait, like my great-great-aunt Rose," she assured him.

"Well, I don't think I can stand the thought of you pining away." He got down on one knee on the concrete, uncaring of his elegant pant leg. "Marry me, Danny. I swear I'll never be gone as long as your great-great-uncle."

He slipped a ring from his pocket and gently slid it on her finger.

Dana looked down at it and gasped. It was a size too big, but it was also antique gold set with an exquisite emerald the size of a marble.

"Is it real?" she asked, looking straight up into his eyes.

"Danny, Penny and I found Abbott's treasure. It was on the mountain face stashed in a cave behind the cross. There was a small chest of doubloons and a few other interesting pieces of jewelry."

"I can't believe it!" She stared at it as she held up her hand to the light. She started to take it off and he stopped her.

"One way or another, I wanted you to have this.

Penny and I both did. You were the first one to see the cross. It's your share of the booty," he told her with a grin.

Eyes that he found more beautiful than the large emerald in the treasure ring smiled back at him. "Yes, Jeff. Yes, I do want to marry you."

She reached out to his shoulders and drew him to her, laying her mouth against his until he wasn't sure where he was or why he was kneeling on cold cement.

"I love you, Jeff."

"I love you, Danny." He touched a tear that rolled slowly down her cheek. "Of course, now I'll never know if you really love me for myself or for my money."

He stood up and took her hand to help her to her feet.

"That's true." She swept her gaze up and down the long length of him. "And when we're on our honeymoon, and when we're celebrating our first anniversary, and our fiftieth, you still won't know, will you?"

She walked past him into the lighted foyer where her family waited patiently.

Jeff smiled with anticipation at the vivid image she'd planted in his mind, and wondered when the next flight left for Wilmington.